To my

Prologue

"I don't even think I've had my first kiss yet, John," I mocked. Tony, Luca, and myself were playing *Never Have I Ever* on *The Review with John Feton*, and he had asked us if we had ever been in a relationship before. Well, of course, Tony and Luca have been in one before, but I have not. I'm not sure why I haven't, perhaps it is because boys find my face weird? I'm not really sure, and to be quite frank, I don't really care. John shot a look that clearly stated that he did not believe me, but it was true. "Oh, wow," he breathed in shock. "Tony and Luca, would you guys ever let somebody date Giovanna?"

"No," They both said in unison. They have always been so protective of me as if I am their litter sister.

"Well then, do you have a celebrity crush, Giovanna?" I just blushed and shook my head and stared down at the fabric of my blood red dress I was wearing. There was no way in hell that I was going to admit to everyone on live television that I have a huge crush on Niall Horan. I know that he doesn't even know who I am, who Insieme is, even though we get swarmed with paparazzi as soon as we step foot onto the streets. However, I know that John is pretty close with him and I don't want to take any chances.

To be fair, I guess that you could say that we became "famous" by accident. John was showing the video of Insieme singing in my uncle's restaurant, and that was the video that really started our career.

"Hey, it's okay, you can tell everybody, Gia," Tony teased as he placed his hand on my shoulder. He clearly wanted to embarrass me infront of millions of people, and I was in no mood for his drama tonight.

"Okay, Tony, let's talk about your-"
BRING BRING.

I shot up in bed. The painful sound of my alarm clock brings me back to reality. There was no Tony or Luca sitting next to me all dressed up in suits and I was not in a flattering dress. I was in my tank-top and shorts, in my bed holding my teddy bear close. I let out a big groan as I shut off my alarm. It was just a dream. It will always be just a dream, and I hated that.

Chapter 1

"What takes you so long to get ready in the morning, Gia. You're going to be late for school," my mother scolded me as she handed me a cold protein shake. I did not want to explain to her that I was dreading going to school because I would much rather be with Tony and Luca. I guess I wouldn't be with them, considering the fact that I haven't seen them in about a year now.

"Do you think that this much beauty is easy to maintain?" I laughed and pointed to myself. That was the one habit that I could not break; I always hid my hurting with jokes and laughter. Sometimes it's a good attribute to have, but it also puts a little bit of a strain on my relationship with others because I can be closed-off.

I chugged down the disgusting spinach protein shake my mother had made me before sprinting up the stairs to fix my hair. I looked into the bathroom mirror and was taken aback. My parents and family friends tell me that I am gorgeous, but when I look in the mirror I just see a hideous girl staring back at me. My nose is too wide and takes up the majority of my face, my left eye is slightly bigger than my right, my legs were much too big for my slim waist, and on top of that, my hip dips were bluntly in your face. I was dressed in my favourite pair of light wash skinny jeans and tight fitting long sleeve black shirt. I refuse to wear short sleeve shirts to school because the flabby fat on the back of my arms squish whenever I sit down. My hair, oh my hair, the long curly mess nest of hair. My dark brown curls lay just beneath my shoulders, and to be quite honest, I think my hair is beautiful except in the mornings. I violently brushed through my thick hair and groaned a little in pain before I slicked it all back into two medium sized pig tails.

I placed both of my hands on the countertop and took a deep breath. I wanted to stop hating my body, after all it was exhausting and I had already dropped thirty pounds because I've started to workout almost every day, but I just couldn't. Perhaps I can't stop hating my appearance because of the hurtful things others have said, or maybe it's because of all the rude things the models at my old junior high school had said to me. Regardless, I just want to feel loved.

I looked at my clock and realized that I only had ten minutes to walk to school before the first bell rang. I quickly packed my things in my grey backpack and grabbed my earbuds before dashing out the door. I loved walking to high school, it gives me a chance to prepare myself for whatever the day ahead might bring me. I would always mentally prepare myself to face Sonia, even though everytime I see her I just cower in my skin. She always has something bad to say about me and she's the worst part of social class. I also prepare myself and brainstorm ideas of what I should say to Danny. Danny is the cute brunette with puppy dog eyes who sits next to me in science class. Despite all of the preparing I do on my five minute walk to school, I end up choking on my words whenever he talks to me. I know that he will probably never like me, but I allow my mind to wander down the paths of thoughts that lead to the possibility of the two of us together.

"Giovanna!" I jumped up in shock as I yanked my earbuds out. Jana was calling me over; she always waits for me outside of the building so we can walk to french class together. We made small talk as we passed through the crowded hallways, holding onto each other's hands for dear life as we always do because we are barely five feet tall and we get crushed in the halls.

"Are you actually going to talk to Danny today?" She asked me as we both got our french notes out.

"We talk everyday," I countered. It was true, though, and we even text on the weekends sometimes.

"No, I meant that you guys should ask each other out, rather than just talking about science questions."

I dropped my mouth so it would take shape in the form of a circle. "We don't just talk about science! We talk about other things, too."

"Oh, yeah." She raised her eyebrow and dropped her head. "Like what?"

"We talk about sports." Sports. The only thing that keeps me going in life. I love football, in fact, I have a wall dedicated to my Green Bay Packers merchandise in my room. It was the only thing that I talked about with any guy because it is the only topic that I am truly confident in. My legs might be too big and my smile might be too lopsided, but at least I could sit through any sports game and not get lost once. American football is my favourite, but I have nothing against baseball, hockey, basketball, and I will even watch golf.

"Can you guys just shut up and date already," she groaned. I love her. I was about to explain that although I like the idea of being with Danny, I was not prepared to get into a relationship after my previous experience with boys, when our french teacher walked in and started the lesson. I try very hard in french class, but it is still a struggle for me to grasp the basic concepts of conjugating verbs. I often get my Italian mixed up with my French, and my teacher usually gets mad at me, but at least she thinks I am funny. Time goes by so slowly in that class, though, but before I knew it, the bell pierced through the halls to let all the students know to get to their next class. Jana gave me a reassuring smile before we parted ways because she knew I was about to go to science. I hate that class, and if it were up to me I would skip science everyday, but I really wanted to see Danny.

"Hey," Danny said as soon as I reached my desk, causing me to go weak in the knees.

"Hey," I responded as I flashed him the brightest smile I could muster.

"Did you see the Blue Jays game last night?"

"Of course, I would never miss any of their games, I love them." *Shut up, Gia, just try and be cool* I thought to myself as we continued to talk about every inning of the ball game in depth. I loved how he knew all my favourite players, but that caused the butterflies to come alive in my stomach.

"What's up, Danny," Conner asked in his annoying high pitched voice. I could not stand Conner and I'm not sure why Danny is friends with him. We talked about it briefly the other day, and he said it is because they've played basketball together ever since they were little boys, but I still can't stand him. He is the definition of a stereotypical highschool player, he is the complete opposite of Danny. Conner wears his hat too high up on his head and pounces intentionally as he takes every step, and he uses basketball slang that I don't understand half of the time.

Danny, on the other hand, is the strong, silent type. I don't talk to Danny as much when Conner is around simply because I can't stand Conner, and now I was silently pretending to be focused on my science homework. The class went by quicker than I expected, but that meant that I was off to social class and I would have to see Sonia.

As soon as I walked into the social room, I spotted Allie, my favourite person ever. She is the sweetest person in this class, and we are always partners, and she always stands up for me whenever I lose my voice when I'm talking to Sonia. Thankfully, Sonia was not here today, allowing me to enjoy Social Studies without her constantly judging me.

The end of the day came quicker than I had expected, but now it was spring break. I was happy that I would get two full weeks off without having to worry about assignments, but I was sad that I would not see Danny. I know it is silly of me to constantly want to be around him, but he just makes me happier, and I hope he can say the same about me.

I took the scenic route home, listening to my One Direction playlist, the sweet sound of their beautiful voices taking all my worries away.

When I opened the door to my house, my dad was quick to embrace me into a tight hug. He was a hugger when it came to family, but not with anyone else. I said hello to my mother and explained to the both of them how my day was and I asked them about how the business was doing.

My parents own a business together, it is kind of funny because they bought the business before they bought their first house. They operate their office from our personal home, so yes, when I am trying to take a nap I usually get woken up by the business phone ringing.

Overall, our house is pretty lively. There's always music playing-my dad usually puts it on- we host guests a lot, my brother and I bring friends over, so safe to say there is never a dull moment in the Rossi household. My brother, Antonio, is in grade twelve, and we both attend the same high school. Antonio and I have always been inseparable; we're best friends. I really do love my family, even when we get into unnecessary fights.

My brother's going onto University soon, and me? Well I don't know, I've never really specialized in anything.

  After I finished all my homework, I refused to do it at school because I would prefer to distract all my classmates. I went downstairs to my family's home gym. Working out was one of my coping mechanisms; it was one of those things that made me forget about all of my problems. My gym was like my little escape; I thought about nothing but using the correct form for my deadlifts.

  Eventually, sadly, I finished the workout and went to shower, blasting Rihanna as loud as my speaker dared. This seemed to be my routine everyday, go to school, do homework, eat dinner with my family, two days a week I go to dance, do even more homework, go downstairs and workout, shower, and then finally go into the family room to watch a show with my whole family. We finally finished our show and we all went to bed around 10:00pm. I know, pretty boring and basic, but after 10:00pm was my favorite time of day. It was the only time of day where nobody was watching, where I could listen to music loudly in my earbuds without having to worry in a world because I knew that no one could see me. In the nighttime, I become a free person.

Chapter 2

As much as I tried to force myself to fall asleep, I was wide awake with one thing on my mind: Insieme. I wondered why Tony and Luca popped up in my dream out of nowhere, and I became sad at the thought of not being able to see them until another big banquet gets scheduled. I couldn't help but think that I had that dream for a reason, but I kept reminding myself that it was silly of me. It was silly of me to think that I would ever sell out stadiums, let alone ever talk to the boys. Maybe if I gained even just a pinch of confidence, but I don't know.

Sure, I've always wanted something more than this life. Of course I'm grateful for all that life has given me thus far, but I just feel as though I'm stuck in the same routine. I want to go out there and explore the world and have strangers call out my name whenever I step onto the street or onto the stage.

I sulked in my room for about an hour before I decided to FaceTime my best friend.

"What's up," Mary grumbled as soon as she picked up the call.

"Were you sleeping?" I asked, instantly feeling bad that I woke her up, but it was still early in the night so I thought she would still be awake.

"Gia, of course I'm sleeping at 2am in the morning." She sounded annoyed, but now she was smiling and I took that as a good sign. *Had I really been thinking about Insieme for that long?* I wondered.

"Are we still on for Lane's tomorrow?"

"Of course." Lane's is the local burger place Mary and I go to all the time. Sure, it was not the healthiest of choices, but we all deserve a reward once in a while. And by once in a while I really mean once every two weeks. Mary and I have been best friends ever since I joined the local Italian Folk Dancer group here in Calgary. We clicked instantly, it was like she was destined to be my sister. We share the same interest in One Direction, and we end up falling onto our rear ends at dance and laughing our heads off. Of course I love all the other girls on my team, but Mary is my best friend. Although we've only known each other for about two years now, we are inseparable. We even teach the smallest group in the dance club together. Mary and I go to different schools, but we still manage to keep touch and fill each other in on whatever new gossip is going on.

"Did you talk to Danny today?" Yes, I told Mary every small detail about all my encounters with the boy in my science class. I filled her in on our talk about the baseball game, even though she knew nothing about baseball and didn't understand a word I said. We talked for about two hours before we ended the call and I fell asleep, pulling my multicoloured teddy bear, who I called Groovy Bear, close to my chest for comfort.

"Took you long enough," Mary scoffed when I approached the picnic table she had reserved for us. She had already got my order of a medium burger and onion rings; she knew me well.

"Sorry, I was walking my dog," I explained, instantly tearing off the paper wrapped around my greasy burger.

"I can't believe we still have to go in for dance class this week when everybody is on spring break," she complained as she rolled her eyes.

"I agree, I think that we all deserve time off."

"At least we don't have school to worry about, but I guess you're sad about that because you won't see Danny."

I blushed and nearly choked on the onion ring that was halfway down my throat. "You got me there." We talked about the new dance we were in the process of making when we were interrupted

"Giovanna?" An all too familiar voice uttered behind me.

No. That can't be.

Chapter 3

"Tony?" I stuttered as I spun around to face him. Standing in front of me was a 5'6 dark haired boy. My heart started to speed up as I thought back to my dream I had a few nights ago, which caused me to stare at him like a deer in the headlights. I was so stunned that I barely spat out a goodbye to Mary when she told me that her mother had arrived.

"How have you been?" He asked as he made his way over to the seat that was once Mary's.

"I've been good, how are you?" I tried to make my voice sound like it normally would, but it sounded like somebody had a grasp on my throat.

"I've been alright. You know how high school can be." I nodded slowly, still distracted from the fact that this could be the boy I spend the rest of my life with making music. I pondered if I should tell him my dream, but then I reminded myself that he would think that I am completely crazy and out of my mind. We barely speak to each other. Sure, we are friendly at functions, and we text each other occasionally, but that's about it. What was I supposed to say? That I want him to be in a trio with Luca and myself, Luca isn't even here right now.

"Are you alright, Giovanna?"

"Tony, I have to tell you something," I breathed as I tried to calm myself down. I figured that I had nothing to lose if I told him about a simple dream, and I knew that if I didn't at least tell him, I would regret it for the rest of my life.

"You're scaring me now," he chuckled nervously, but I could see the concerned look spread across his face.

"I had a dream, and you were in it," I blurted out. Tony shot me a puzzled expression, so I quickly carried on, "It was nothing romantic or anything like that." He smiled and nodded, and I let out a laugh. "Have you ever heard of *The Review with John Fenton*?" He nodded with big eyes. "Well, you, myself, and Luca were on that show getting interviewed by him. We were in a famous singing trio called Insieme and we were playing *Never Have I Ever*. He asked if we had ever been in a relationship before and I, of course, said that I had never been in one." He started to laugh because he knew my luck was slim to none when it came to relationships. I rolled my eyes as I continued, "Very funny. Anyway, you almost told everybody on the show my celebrity crush, and I was about to tell them an embarrassing story, but then I woke up." Tony was silent for a moment, and I could feel the worry in my body start to swell up.

"How did we end up on the show?" He sounded interested, so I took that as a good sign.

"Oh, I forgot that part, sorry. John showed a little clip of our most viral video. We were singing in my uncle's restaurant and it got hundreds of thousands of views." We sat in silence for what felt like infinity, and then he reached across the table and grabbed my wrist. I had no choice but to stand up and follow him wherever he was planning on taking me. "Where are we going?"

"My mom's here." He was charging towards the parking lot, and I stopped on my heels. He wiped his head around to see what was going on.

"Why are you taking me with you?"

"Well, Luca was going to come over anyway so I'm taking you with me," he explained impatiently as if I should already have known this.

"Why?" I asked, but I started following him into his mother's car.

"To tell Luca about your dream."

The car ride to Tony's house was awkward to say the least. He tried to make small talk and his mother was trying to ask me questions about how dance is going. I, however, was not interested in either of them. I know that it is rude and that I should be polite, but I was trying to wrap my brain around the thought of Insieme actually coming together. I was nervous, that must be why my leg was bouncing up and down uncontrollably, but I was also excited because maybe the boys would want this.

After a painfully long car ride to his house, we were parked on his driveway. As soon as I got out of the car I spotted Luca standing at Tony's doorstep.

"Giovanna?"

"Hey." My heart raced faster than a Formula1 race car as I saw Luca walk towards me.

"Everyone to the basement right now," Tony demanded, and Luca and I shared a funny glance, but we did not argue with him. "Giovanna, explain to Luca why you are here with us," Tony said as soon as we were all sitting on the couch.

"I don't know why I'm here," I giggled to Luca, causing Tony to groan. "Quit whining."

"Tell him about your dream!" Tony was very passionate about this dream. I did as he asked, leaving not even a single detail out of the dream I had. Tony was beaming from ear to ear, but Luca was staring back at me with a blank expression after I had told him what my dream was.

"I think we should do it," Tony shrugged, catching me off guard. I was not quite sure if I could even sing in tune, but Tony did not seem to mind.

"Me too," Luca agreed, saying something for the first time since we got to the basement. That was easy. "Are you in, Gia?"

What a great question, was I in? After all, it was my dream, but I was still scared. What if people don't like us, or more specifically if they don't like me. If we end up going viral then maybe people will comment on my weird body shape and my disproportionate facial features.

"Giovanna?" Tony asked as if I did not hear Luca the first time. I glanced at the boys who were both wearing hopeful smiles. The sparkle in Luca's eyes said it all.

"I'm in."

The boys let out a collective sigh as they let their shoulders drop in relief. I couldn't help but smile. I was so wrapped up in my thoughts that I almost did not notice Luca dialling the number to my uncle's restaurant.

"Shouldn't you be the one on the phone because your uncle might say no to Luca but he won't say no to you," Tony whispered. I just shrugged, relieved that I would not have to talk on the phone. I hate talking on the phone, I always feel like the person on the other line is judging me and I somehow manage to pronounce all of the words that came out of my mouth wrong.

"May I speak to the owner, please?" Luca asked. "Yes, I can wait." He stared at us, and then I realized that this was happening all too fast.

"Luca hang up," I said, trying to sound as intimidating as possible. Both of the boys gave me a confused look and Luca was still on hold. "Luca end the call right now." The words came out harsher than I had expected, but we were simply not ready to perform together yet.

"Hi, this is Luca, Luca-" before he had the chance to introduce himself I had leaped across the room and snatched the phone right out of his hand.

"Sorry, wrong number," I said quickly, hanging up before I waited for a response. I gasped for air because I was slightly out of shape from the burger that was yet to digest in my stomach and looked up at the boys. They were even more dumbfounded than before, and I honestly had no idea what to say to them.

"What was that about?" Luca asked, and the hurt in his voice was apparent.

"Look, guys, of course, I want this dream of mine to come true," I began.

"Could have fooled me," Luca scoffed quietly under his breath.

"But hear me out," I reasoned, choosing to ignore Luca's tone. "We haven't even so much as sang a simple karaoke song together, so why would we call the restaurant? We need to take this slowly and make sure that we sound good together." As much as I hated seeing the pain on Luca's face, I was standing my ground because I was logical.

"You're right," Luca whispered quietly, purposely looking anywhere but my eyes. Tony was about to say something, but his mother called him upstairs because she needed to talk to him, leaving Luca and myself alone.

"I'm sorry, I shouldn't have yanked the phone away from you," I apologized. I was genuinely sorry, and I could understand why Luca would be mad at me, but instead of yelling at me, Luca had started to cry. I could see the tears stroll down his face, and I became instantly uncomfortable. I had only been here for an hour, and I had somehow managed to make him cry. Great job, Giovanna.

"I'm not mad at you," Luca mustered up through tears, but he did not sound convincing whatsoever. "It's just that I really want this to happen." I scooched closer to him and cautiously placed my arm around his shoulder in hopes that it would somehow comfort him. I am so bad around people who cry, I become very awkward and weird and just genuinely useless, but Luca seemed to calm down a little.

"I was wrong, I'm sorry." It was the only thing that I could think of to say, and I wished that I could come up with something better. Luca sat there in my arms, crying until there were no tears left to cry, before Tony came back down.

"I'm sorry, but you guys need to go," he huffed, trying to catch his breath at the same time. "My Aunt Lidia is coming over tonight, and apparently we need to get ready."

If there was one thing that I knew for certain about Tony, it is that he could not stand his Aunt Lidia. He claims that she is too pushy and always has her nose in other people's business.

"Can we come over tomorrow?" Luca asked.

"Yeah, of course, let's meet at my house around 3pm," Tony said. I felt bad that I sort of invited myself, well to be fair, it was Luca's idea, but I did not protest.

The three of us helped Tony clean up before our parents arrived. All of our moms were chatting about a new sale at a local shop, and the boys and myself were discussing the details for tomorrow. Once our parents were finally done talking about the new sales, I waved goodbye to Tony and Luca and was in the car. My mother was about to ask me how my day was, but she got a call from her sister and was on the phone with her the whole ride home, leaving me to sit there in silence. I wanted nothing more than to just go home and take a nice long shower, but my mother was driving as slow as possible.

After what should have been a twenty minute drive but took forty minutes, I was finally home. I grabbed my phone, it was lit up with messages from all my friends but I was in no mood to text anybody at the moment. I turned the shower knob to the on position and waited for the water to warm up. I opened my music app and selected my playlist, hit shuffle, and then hopped into the warm shower. The shower was always a place where I would sing and think about what was going on in my life right now. I thought that maybe a shower would help me collect my thoughts, process what was going on, but it didn't. I ended up just kind of standing there awkwardly examining the patterned white tiles on the wall. I rinsed the oat scented shampoo out of my thick hair and applied my conditioner. I sang the first line of *Fool's Gold* by One Direction and I clasped my hands to my mouth. *Did I just effortlessly sing, in tune, with One Direction?* Usually, I am way out of tune, either too sharp or too flat, however; it was a heavenly sound that escaped my lips tonight. I shocked myself. I always sang in the shower, but now that Luca, Tony and I wanted to be famous, I was really listening to see how my voice sounded. I grabbed the bar of soap off of the ledge and continued singing along to one of my favorite songs. I hit the high notes with ease, shocking myself. I let out a big laugh, maybe this whole singing thing could work out after all.

Chapter 4

"Goodnight, I love you." I gave my parents both a quick peck on the cheek before heading to my bedroom. I scrolled through my phone, but I did not have the energy to answer all of the text messages people had sent me. I'm the worst person to have a conversation with over text messages because I would much rather talk face-to-face, and that is why I rarely answer people. Another reason, now, is that Insieme was on my mind. More specifically, Luca was on my mind.

Luca and I have known each other ever since I can remember, but we have never been that close. We know each other on a deeper level than just mutual friends, but I've never had him cry on my shoulder before. He was not usually the type to cry, he's known for being the tough star football player, but then again, we never really know somebody's true feelings.

I was tossing and turning, trying to fall asleep so that tomorrow I would not have dark circles under my eyes, but I just could not get comfortable. I was about to open up the Solitaire app because that usually helps me fall asleep, when I heard my phone make a *ding* noise and I saw Luca's name pop up.

Luca: Hey, are you awake?

Me: Yeah, I can't sleep. What's up?

Luca: Me too, I feel bad that I broke down in front of you today and I just wanted to say sorry.
I let out a big sigh, a little bit too loudly, and my thumbs hovered over my phone. *What should I say?*

Me: Luca, it is totally okay. Don't feel bad, just know that I am here for you and I will always listen to you. I am so sorry for taking the phone away from you. If you ever need to talk you can always come to me.

I hit send and stared at the three little dots that popped up as he was typing. Two minutes later my phone buzzed.

Luca: *You did the right thing by taking the phone away from me, I should have listened to you sooner. I don't really know what came over me at Tony's today though. I usually don't cry in front of people, I guess I just feel really comfortable around you. I am so stressed from the upcoming football season, I mean of course I like football, but people just think I'm only good at football. Whenever they think of me they just automatically associate me with football, and I'm more than just a game. As far as your dream, I want to make sure it comes true. I know that if maybe we can get a shot at singing, people will view me as more than just a dumb football player.*

Me: *Luca I had no idea you felt that way. I have seen you played here and there, and you really do have a talent for football. If it makes any difference, I don't view you as a "dumb football player." I see you as someone who makes sacrifices for those he loves, you're sweet, understanding, patient, and so funny, and I hope you know that you are so talented. I've heard you sing before, and you have such an angelic voice. I'm here for you Luca :)*

I closed the messages to switch my playlist, but when I came back my screen read: seen two minutes ago. *Uh oh, maybe he thought I had a crush on him,* which I don't, *or maybe he just wanted a shorter response, what do I-* My train of thought was cut off by an incoming FaceTime call from Luca. I smiled stupidly at my phone as I flicked my lamp on and pressed the answer icon.

He seemed surprised when I picked up the call and started laughing, I let out a big laugh of my own and we ended up laughing for a solid five minutes together.

"Let me add Tony to the call," Luca said in between laughs.

Maybe I was just sleep deprived, but that made me laugh even harder.

"Guys, what the hell!" Tony demanded as soon as he joined the call. Luca burst out laughing, making me belly laugh harder.

"It is 1:30 am, why are we calling each other?" He asked. Luca responded for me while I attempted, but failed, to catch my breath.

"I texted Giovanna to see if she was awake, and she was so then we were texting because we couldn't fall asleep so I just called her," he explained as he petted his small dog.

"You guys, I am exhausted from my Aunt, okay? Is this necessary?" He asked, clearly annoyed.

I piped up, "You can leave the call then," I laughed again. "We just wanted to include you." Luca was taking a drink from his glass, but I made him laugh so hard he spat out his water. Tony shook his head and placed his phone on his desk.

"You know what, Gia, your dream isn't going to work out if you keep giving me this attitude," he said, but he lightened his tone and I saw the corners of his mouth curl up. It has always been hard for Tony to be mad for a long period of time; he was a softie on the inside. We talked about football, my dance group, Tony's new film he was making for a project, and how everyone has been doing in high school since we were all freshmans. We talked for about an hour before I started yawning and then Tony made the suggestion to continue our conversation tomorrow when we were all together.

"Goodnight, you guys," Tony whispered.

"Goodnight, everyone," I murmured back.

"Goodnight, I love you guys, " Luca hushed, and Tony and I said it back to him with smiles plastered onto our faces.

Chapter 5

I awoke the next morning with sunshine beating in through my blinds. My stomach was churning with nervousness as I made my way to the washroom. I stared at myself in the mirror and instantly regretted staying up late to talk to the boys. Deep dark circles laid underneath my eyes, and my meditiranniean skin tone was now pasty white. I looked disheveled, as usual, but today was especially worse.

"Hurry up, Giovanna, we are going to be late!" My dad called from downstairs. I scurried to the stairwell with a perplexed look.

"I'm not supposed to be at Tony's until 3?"

"Yeah, exactly," my dad said, growing slightly impatient. "You slept in until 1:55 in the afternoon and we need to get a move on." Shit. I guess I stayed up a little too late talking to the boys last night, but I had no time to sulk about the fact that I would be going to Tony's house on an empty stomach. I quickly went back to my room and changed into my white romper with a brown belt built into the waistband of it. It gave me somewhat of an hourglass figure, accentuating my curves and hiding the hip dips underneath the loose fitting fabric. My naturally curly hair fell flawlessly beneath my shoulders, and I was feeling a little prettier than I had when I first caught sight of myself. I did not have much time to look at myself in the mirror, which I did not mind, before my dad called my name again and before I knew it we were in his truck.

We were listening to *What Makes You Beautiful* by One Direction, my dad's favourite song of theirs, while my dad zipped in between various cars. As much as I love One Direction, I am convinced that my father loves them even more. He even bought their debut album when it first came out, and he refuses to listen to any other CD when we are driving together, which I do not mind whatsoever.

"We need to talk," my dad said, turning down the radio once his favourite song was over. I could feel my leg start to bounce as I started to get nervous.

"What's up?" I tried to sound calm, but my voice came out shaky.

"I heard you talking on FaceTime last night," he started, and my first thought was that I would be getting my phone taken away for being too loud. "I heard you guys talking about wanting to potentially pursue a career in singing." He paused, making my leg bounce rapidly. "I've heard you sing, Gia, and I think you have a beautiful voice."

"Thank you," I peeped. The compliment really did mean a lot to me, but I just could not find the right words to say.

"You're welcome, and I want you to know that that is the reason why I am letting you sleep over tonight." What. The same guy who would not let me go out on a simple coffee date with a boy is going to let me sleepover at Tony's house? I can wake up from the dream now.

"Before you start asking a million questions," he continued. "I already talked to Tony's mom when you were sleeping and she is completely okay with it. She thinks that Insieme is a wonderful name for you guys and she said that you can ask her for anything if you need something."

"Thanks dad." But what would I wear? I did not bring a change of clothes, and did the boys even know that I would be spending the night with them? Before I had a chance to ask my dad any questions, we were already on Tony's driveway.

"Let me be clear," he cleared his throat. "If I hear that you caused any trouble, you will get grounded. Don't make me regret this."

"I won't," I promised.

"Now," he smiled. "Go have fun, I love you."

"I love you, dad."

And with that I was already ringing Tony's doorbell, my dad had already taken off and I was now alone eagerly waiting for Tony to answer the door.

"Gia's here!" Tony screamed over his shoulder. "Come on in, Giovanna."

He was wearing a pair of blue levi jeans with a jet black button up shirt. His black hair was slicked back and his eyes were beaming with hope. I always thought Tony had a good fashion sense, he never showed up in just a plain T-shirt, he was always dressed up. Tony embraced me into a tight hug, I thought he was going to choke me. I gave a nervous laugh and then I heard footsteps coming from the flight of stairs leading to the basement.

Luca appeared with his pearly white teeth grinning widely at me. He was wearing a pair of black jeans with a plain white t-shirt tucked into them and an opened button up baby blue shirt laid perfectly on his shoulders. I let out a laugh because last night I said that an outfit like that was my favourite thing a boy could wear. I thought the look was kind of business-casual, and Luca really did pull off the look.

"We've been waiting," Luca said with a smirk as he pulled me in for a hug. He was quite a bit taller than me, so my head ended up near his shoulders. I could smell the faint smell of his tobacco cologne bleeding through his shirt.

"I'm sorry to keep you guys waiting, but you guys both know I live in the south part of the city. Besides, you guys live in the same neighbourhood," I stated, untangling myself from Luca's arms.

"Sure, make excuses," Tony rolled his eyes. "Let's go downstairs and start picking out songs to cover."

Tony was already sprinting down the stairs, I quickly followed him but Luca tugged my arm stopping me in mid stride. "Sorry, didn't mean to scare you," he chuckled and I relaxed slightly, "I just wanted to know if you liked my outfit today."

I probably would have said yes because it was a pretty nice outfit, but he winked at me when he was done talking and I just rolled my eyes so far back I swear I saw my brain, mocked his wink and continued downstairs shaking my head.

"What does Insieme mean?" Tony asked us once we were all sitting down in a half circle on his carpet floor. His eyebrow was raised up slightly, although all three of us are Italian, he spoke the least Italian out of all of us.

Luca scoffed at Tony; he knew the language really well because he's enrolled in a class. In fact, he is so good at speaking the language that he was in the grade eleven class. I hit him on the side of his arm, there was no need to make Tony feel bad.

"Sorry," Tony mumbled, but a smile still remained on his face.

"*Insieme* means 'together'," I explained. "It means to unite and come together. It's a beautiful name for a trio, really. It has meaning, like we are all united together and singing with passion."

"Hmm interesting," Tony said, staring off into the distance. "Do you really think non-Italians will be able to say that word though?"

It was a fair point, I was about to agree with him but Luca piped up, "I really like it. Plus, we can explain to people the meaning behind it, and if we say it enough in interviews or YouTube videos, eventually people will be able to say it properly." He smiled proudly when the three of us all nodded in agreement.

The three of us all had a bottle of Pepsi in our hands, that was the only kind of pop that Tony had. He always preached about how if he could only drink one beverage for the rest of his life, it would be Pepsi. I enjoyed it as well, but I was not nearly as passionate about it as Tony was. Luca seemed to enjoy it as well, but he never gave his opinion on it.

"Do you think we could start singing?" Luca urged. As soon as he said that my right leg started bouncing uncontrollably. I've always been a little bit insecure about how I sing, some people might not think that it's good. I have always struggled in taking the first step, I always seem to need a little nudge of reassurance before I start something new. I knew the boys would be supportive of me no matter what I sound like, but I guess I just don't want to let anybody down.

Tony's gaze landed on my leg, I wanted my leg to stop bouncing but I could not control it. "Hey, don't worry, Giovanna. We're all going to sing a song for each other individually, and then we can start working on singing together." Tony gave me a reassuring nod as he finished, it seemed to calm me down a little bit, but I was still nervous.

"I'll go first!" Luca stated excitedly, winking as he said it.

I completely lost it, "Luca stop winking!" I said in between laughter. The three of us all started laughing and the nervous feeling that I once had faded away. I felt comfortable, and my leg was even planted firmly on the ground. Luca sprang to his feet and started to type in a song into Tony's karaoke machine.

Tony's family loved karaoke, they were always throwing karaoke parties, and it was their family tradition for the birthday person to get up and sing a song at their party.

Luca inhaled deeply from his diaphragm before he belted out the words to Queen's *Somebody to Love*. The piano started playing after Luca effortlessly hit all the right notes with a proud smile across his face. He continued singing the famous Queen song and his performance made Tony and I's jaw drop. Luca sang with such passion, yet it was easy for him to vocalize. The words flowed off his tongue carelessly; he really did have a true talent. The song lasted for about four minutes before he hit a long whistle note that made Tony and I clap our hands together. His eyes were closed when he sang, but when he opened them I could see the sparkle in his eyes. His eyes were filled with hope, happiness, and a longing for something more than his current life. I could tell that Luca really wanted to be a singer, I no longer saw a future CFL player, I saw someone who allowed themselves to be vulnerable.

Tony and I both explained to Luca that he had a pure talent and that he has a beautiful singing voice. Luca said that we were being too kind, but we insisted that we were being completely honest with him. Luca's cheeks turned as red as tomatoes as he thanked us for all the compliments we just showered him with.

"I did it, your turn Tony." He nudged Tony on the shoulder and made his way next to me on the coach. Tony looked a bit uneasy, but he eventually picked up the microphone, cussing quietly under his breath while he tried to pick out a song. Luca and I gave each other a confused look.

"You alright?" I asked.

Tony looked up and spat out, "Yeah, I'm alright I just don't know what to sing."

"Well, just pick the first song that comes to mind." I knew it was not that great of advice, but he had to pick the song, Luca and I could not pick for him. Eventually, the start of *Wonderwall* echoed out of the machine.

It was like hearing an angel, he was right in tune and on time. It was a classic song, but it fit his voice perfectly. He got really into it, letting his hands fly around, he was a natural performer. It was like Tony had been born to be on stage, maybe his drama class helped with stage presence, but he was really good at maintaining the audience's

44

attention. After about three minutes, the Oasis song stopped and Luca and I were applauding him.

Tony thanked the both of us as we were telling him how great of a job he just did. He wore a proud grin that covered the width from each of his cheeks. I could tell that Tony liked performing, in fact, both of them were natural at performing. I could feel my leg starting to bounce again, my palms were sweaty and sticking to my bare legs. I could feel my heart pound viscously in my chest.

"You're up, Gia!" they said in unison.

I don't know how I could possibly go after those two performances. They were both so talented, and I'm just, well I'm just mediocre. Luca squeezed my shoulder as he nodded toward the karaoke machine. I gulped, *it's now or never.*

Chapter 6

Everything disappeared, I saw nothing but the microphone. There was nobody else in the room, it was just me and the black microphone. The boys were cheering me on, but they were just background noise at this point.

Paper Houses is one of my favourite Niall Horan songs to sing. I knew all the words so I didn't even have to follow along with the words displayed on the screen. I could hear the boys gasp in shock, and I don't know what came over me but I belted out the chorus.

A rush of adrenaline washed over me, it was like I had left my body. I had no control over my actions; it was like I was not Giovanna anymore. For the first time in a long time, a sense of pride washed over me. My eyes were open, but I saw nothing, everything was a blur, and all I could hear was the words roll off of my tongue smoothly.

After about roughly three and a half minutes the music slowly faded out. I stood there gripping the microphone tightly in my hand, my heart was pounding and my stomach was flipping. The boys sat dumbfounded on Tony's sectional, so I stood there in silence pondering my next move.

Maybe I should just leave? I wondered as my head started pounding. I quietly placed the microphone on its stand when Tony started to speak.

"Wow," he mumbled.

That single word, that one single word, made me panic. I started to wonder why they have not yet applauded me, I applauded them. Maybe it was because they thought that I was not that good. Is "Wow" a good reaction, or a bad reaction?

"You sound," Luca started but then shortly closed his mouth after. His brow was creased and I could tell that he was searching for something to say.

"I sound?" I ask, raising my eyebrows in anticipation.

The two of them glanced at each other, and I could feel my heart drop. *They don't want me to be in the trio.* I thought, but I tried hard to push that thought away to the back of my mind.

"You sound sensational," Luca finally cracked.

All of my worries dissipated, and a wide grin formed on my face. Tony nodded his head in agreement and before I knew it, the both of them were getting up to hug me. I thanked them profusely as they wrapped their arms around me and sandwiched me in between them. I could not muster up the strength to tell them how much their kindness meant to me, I could only smile and wipe away the tears that started to form in my eyes with the heels of my hands.

At that moment, I felt joy. Not happiness, but rather, joy. I could feel myself come alive. A bolt of energy rushed through my body and I started to ramble to the boys,

"So I think we should start singing as a trio and maybe upload a couple videos to YouTube. What do you guys think?" I was bouncing with excitement.

"I think that is a great idea!" Luca responded, matching my excited energy.

We both stared at Tony, the anticipation was killing me.

"As much as I love singing," he started and I could feel all of the joy rush out of my body, "I think we should get some snacks and play on my PlayStation, and I could even ask my parents if we are allowed to have a few drinks." A mysterious smile spread across his face as he continued, "I mean, we have all night to sing, and I think we should just relax for a couple of hours."

I have to admit that relaxing and playing video games sounded amazing to me right now, so I told him that it was an amazing idea. Luca said that he should call his parents to see if he would be allowed to drink and strolled off into a separate room. Tony rushed upstairs to ask his parents for permission and to grab a few snacks. I realized that I should call my dad, since he trusted me enough to sleep over.

I waited patiently for my dad to pick up on the other line. On the fourth ring my dad finally picked up.

"Hey, Giovanna," he said.

"Hey, Dad! Before you ask, yes I'm okay." I could hear him chuckle, but I also heard a sigh of relief escape his mouth.

"Good, when I saw your name I started to wonder if something went wrong."

"Oh, no, don't worry I was just calling to ask you something." My heart started to race, I knew I was doing the right thing by telling him the truth, but I was still a bit intimidated by my dad and I did not want to push my luck.

"What's up?"

"Tony was wondering if I was allowed to have a drink," I sighed, mentally preparing myself for my dad to explode. There was a long pause before I heard my dad murmur something under his breath that I couldn't quite make out.

"Yes, you are allowed. I trust his parents will limit you, and I also trust that you know your limits. However, if I hear that you did anything stupid because you were tipys, I am coming over and bringing you home. With that being said, I appreciate you calling me and keeping me in the loop. Just please be respectful and responsible, do I make myself clear, Gia?"

I nodded my head as if my dad could somehow see me. Words were not coming out of my mouth; I was shocked at how relaxed my dad was being.

"Giovanna?" He asked with a hint of worry in his tone. I realized that I had never actually responded to him.

"Yes, I'm sorry. I will be responsible, and thank you so much for trusting me. Love you lots, Papa."

"Oh, relax bella, I can hear your smile through the phone," he giggled. "Love you, too, now get off the phone with me and have fun."

I let out a sigh of relief after my dad and I had hung up the phone, I could not believe that this was really happening. First, my dad let me sleepover at a *boys* house. Not only is he letting me sleep over at Tony's, but he is allowing me to have some drinks.

Tony raced down the stairs, tripping over himself in the process, which made Luca emerge from the room in concern. Both of Tony's arms were in the air, and his hands were in the form of a fist.

"My parents are okay if we drink!" He exclaimed, knocking Luca over with his flying arms.

"Oh my goodness!" Luca yelped, a hint of annoyance in his voice as he slowly got up from the floor. "What is the matter with you, Tony?" His voice was stern and his mouth was set in a firm line. I could not tell if he was actually mad at Tony, or if he was just joking. However, Tony was still in his own little bubble, jumping excitedly and rambling on. I could not help myself, and I started to laugh hysterically. My whole body was shaking; I collapsed onto the floor while folding my arms over my stomach.

"What is so funny?" Luca demanded.

"What is the matter with you, Tony?" I mocked in a high pitched voice. Another enormous amount of laughter bursted out of my mouth.

"What is so funny?" Tony mimicked in the same pitched voice as I did. He made his way over to me and plopped down on the carpet. The two of us were uncontrollable. Tears started to roll down my cheeks from laughing so much, and my abs started to cramp a bit. There was a sudden silence that fell over the two of us, but when we gazed at each other we began laughing again.

"Relax, Luca," Tony began in between giggles.

"Yeah, take it easy." I looked at Luca, starting to slowly regain my demeanor. Luca was still standing with his legs spread open and his arms crossed around his chest. I did not understand why he would not take a joke, in fact I could sense that he did not find this even slightly amusing. I sprang to my feet, gliding over towards him hoping that he would ease up. As I approached closer and closer to him, he started to break. I could see the rim of his soft pink lips turn upwards, and his shoulders dropped slightly. It has always been tough for him to stay angry for long periods of time.

"I knew it!" I screamed. "I knew you couldn't stay mad at us!"

A slight smirk spread across his face, "Fine, make fun of me all you guys want." His arms were dangling in the air as if to say he was defeated.

"Oh, we will, don't you worry," Tony teased as he finally made his way towards us. There was a rush of excitement that went through my spine, I was excited about tonight. I was hopeful about what the night would bring, I was hoping that the three of us would harmonize beautifully together. In fact, I was actually nervous for tonight, maybe I would be excluded while the boys just did whatever boys do at sleepovers. However, I realized as the three of us were standing laughing at each other, that we were really like siblings. There was nothing awkward about our hangouts, and I actually felt comfortable around them.

All my life, I've always felt like I had to put on certain different faces to appease people. The only people who really know me are my family, and Mary. I have always been confident in who I am, but I've always felt like I've had to bite back my tongue in many situations in order to please people. Usually, I'm a shy, quiet person, but around these two boys I feel free. They understand me, from our 1am FaceTime calls, to understanding my humour, everything just clicked.

I had a dream all those nights ago, and I, for some reason, decided to be vulnerable and open up to the boys about it. I will admit that I was scared that they would make fun of me and tell me that we will never be famous. I never imagined that they would understand me, and feel the same rage towards our daily routines. Even if we don't end up selling out stadiums and making our own songs, I know that because of that dream, we will have each other's backs for the rest of our lives.

Chapter 7

"No!" Tony exclaimed, slamming his PlayStation controller into the couch. "That's not fair!"

"It's not my fault you don't know how to play Madden," Luca scoffed.

We're playing the NFL game *Madden,* all three of us are big football fans. The two of them were playing each other in a heated match, Luca ended up throwing a thirty-yard touchdown pass in overtime. I thought Tony was going to break down and cry; I will never quite understand why boys take video games so seriously.

"Tony, give me the controller, please. I'll beat Luca since you couldn't," I said looking directly at Luca. Both of them let out a huff, but I eventually got the controller. I picked the Green Bay Packers, and Luca selected his favourite team, the Kansas City Chiefs.

I have a lot of memories attached to this game, in fact, it was the first video game I've ever played on the PlayStation. My brother and I would spend countless hours versing each other, inevitably he would always win; he is the only person who I always lose to, everytime we have guests over I beat everyone who dares to challenge me.

"You ready?" Luca asked.

I shot him a side look and pressed the X button to start the game. There was no way I was losing to a boy, especially Luca.

All of those nights that I would stay up to play Madden finally paid off; I won 35-3. Although I was a little disappointed that I let Luca get a field goal, I was still happy that I did not lose. Luca, on the other hand, was fuming. Even though he did not slam the controller into the coach like Tony had done, he was red in the face and on the verge of yelling at the top of his lungs. As much as I liked Luca, I did not bother to ease up on him.

"Tony, want to play against me?" I questioned as I offered a controller towards him.

"No way, it's a stupid game anyway," He jibed.

I rolled my eyes, certain that if either one of them would have won we would still be playing on the console. Eventually, I gave up and turned off the PlayStation.

"What do you guys want to do now?" Luca
urgered.

"Maybe we could start singing?" I offered,
still a tad upset that we were not playing Madden.

Tony shook his head, "It's a bit early, no?"

I glanced over at the clock hanging on
Tony's beige wall, it was only 10:30 pm.

"Okay, then what should we do?" I pressed.

A quietness fell over the three of us.

"Actually," Luca started, "maybe we could
start singing right now and record it. That way we
can just chill for the remainder of the night and into
the A.M."

That did sound nice, we could get it out of
the way and then relax for a while. I bobbed my
head up and down vigorously. The two of us
glanced at Tony waiting for his response.

"Yeah, that makes the most sense," he
agreed.

The three of us sat in a half circle on the
floor, unsure of what song we should sing.

"I think it is important for us to all have mini
solos, as well as being able to harmonize at certain
parts of the song," Luca stated.

"Yeah, that would be ideal, but what song should we sing?" Tony countered.

It was a good question, and I could not come up with anything. I picked up my phone to start searching through my playlist for a nice song that would suit all of our unique sounding voices. The boys followed suit; all three of us were concentrating on finding the perfect song. I scrolled through my fifteen hour long playlist, searching for a song that would stand out to me. I scrolled past various songs from artists like Madonna, ABBA, and Fleetwood Mac. Nothing seemed to satisfy me.

Desperate to find the perfect song, I picked up my scrolling pace, skimming through my playlist. Suddenly, a One Direction song caught my attention. I was not quite sure how the boys would react to singing a One Direction song, but *Story of My Life* would fit perfectly. We could all sing during the chorus and have our own verses to ourselves. It would work.

"Guys!" I blurted, breaking the silence and making Tony and Luca jump in surprise.

"What?" Tony asked.

"I found the song."

"Well?" Luca questioned impatiently.

"*Story of My Life* by One Direction," I stated proudly.

The two of them stared at me blankly. I could feel my heart start to pound quickly. I knew I should not have said a One Direction song.

"It's perfect," Tony spoke breathlessly.

Luca nodded his head and a slight smile spread across his face. I was reminded, yet again, that when I was with these boys, there was truly no judgement. A warm sensation filled my body as I tried to find the right words to say next.

"Let's get started," I finally said.

In fact, I was a bit relieved that we would finally start recording videos of the three of us. I knew that we were talented, and I knew that we could all bring great aspects to the trio. Luca seemed to be in a rush because he sprang to his feet immediately. It startled Tony a bit, but he followed in Luca's footsteps.

"I'll get my phone set up," Tony claimed.

We're really doing this. I thought to myself, thankful that neither of the boys gave up on my dream.

An hour passed before we finally started to record. We had to pick out parts that best suited each of our voices, and we had to do a few practice runs before we got to recording. I was shocked at how well we harmonized together, it was as if we were born to sing together. Luca sang effortlessly and he sounded amazing, and same with Tony. On the other hand, I had to really focus on breathing through my diaphragm and keeping my throat open in order to sound better. I admit, I was a bit of a liability when we first started singing together. It was always me who was out of tune, or it was me who came in on the wrong count. I don't know how the boys were not furious at me, and maybe they are but they did not show it. I was pleasantly shocked with how patient the two of them were with me.

After a lot of hard work of tweaking little details, we decided we would record a video.

"So we can record on my phone because I already have an account set up with YouTube," Tony offered.

"Sounds good," Luca and I said simultaneously.

Tony set up his camera and asked again if we were ready to record. Finally, he pressed the time button. I could hear the timer clicking down every second that went by. Ten seconds seemed to last an entirety, but my heart started to speed up when the final three seconds appeared on the screen.

A flash of fear came over me, and I considered leaving Tony's house and never speaking to them again. What if I don't sound good? What if we don't even get any views from this video? I was scared. My breathing started to quicken and a cold shiver ran down my spine. I glanced over at Luca, who was standing in the middle of Tony and I, wondering if he was having second thoughts as well. Luca must have picked up on my nervousness because he locked his eyes on mine and squeezed my hand. I started to calm down a little, but my heart was still going faster than a million miles per hour. I was about to tell the boys that I could not go through with this, but Luca breathed in and the words started rolling effortlessly off his tongue.

He started singing the opening verse, letting go of my hand, and I could tell that Luca was in his comfort zone. His eyes shined brightly, his shoulders were relaxed, he seemed to look at ease. I could hear the happiness in his voice as he continued the rest of his dedicated verse. I looked over at Tony, as I knew that his verse was coming up, and when I looked over Tony seemed relaxed as well. Luca stopped singing, and Tony inhaled loudly before his que.

He began, sounding as angelic as ever. Him, too, was in his wheelhouse. He seemed to know exactly what to do with his hands, everything was just natural. I could hear his verse coming to an end, mentally preparing myself to be in tune for the chorus. He stepped back to his original spot during his last line of his verse. I was clearly shaking, but seeing the boys being natural performers gave me a sense of relief. If they could do it, then so could I. The three of us inhaled at once before we belted out the chorus.

We were all perfectly in tune with each other. Everything just fits. Nothing felt forced, and we all sounded amazing. As the chorus started to finish I could feel a spark of excitement throughout my body. I stepped forward, breathing deeply, closed my eyes, only hoping that I would not mess up.

The words flew off my tongue perfectly, shocking myself as I continued to sing. My verse was in time and on-pitch. I could feel myself come alive again, and a sense of hope welling up inside of me.

The three of us sang our hearts out for the remainder of the song. I did not want this feeling to go away, I wanted the song to last forever so this adrenaline could stay with me. After about four minutes, we sang the last line before Tony walked over to stop the video.

Once I heard the click of the recording button turn off, I collapsed to the floor. It was a bit dramatic, but I really did feel like I sang for my life. I laid on my back with my arms spread out like I was making a snow angel. My vision was blurred and I felt tears streaming down my cheeks silently. I knew I should have eaten before I came here.

"What that..." Luca mumbled underneath his breath as he made his way over to me.

"Gia?" Tony asked, equally as concerned as Luca. Tony had just finished uploading our video onto YouTube.

"I'm alright," I assured them, even though I was anything but. To be honest, I was worried as soon as Tony hit the upload button. What would people think of me? Will they think that I ruined the video when I started to sing? I don't know why I was crying, but I guess my hormones were all out of whack.

"You don't seem okay," Luca said, brushing a strand of hair out of my face. I smiled up at him, trying to stop the tears from falling down my face. Tony looked at me sympathetically, but he was busy reloading YouTube.

"I'm just worried."

"About what?" Luca asked gently as he placed his arm around me and I rested my head on his chest.

"It doesn't matter," I whispered, instantly feeling calmness as I sat there in his arms.

I would never date Luca, that would be silly, but he made me feel safe. He seemed to be sympathetic and understanding, but I would never date him. That would just complicate things with Insieme, and I don't want to cause any drama. Plus, I'm still hoping that Danny and I hit it off one of these days, but I know that will never happen.

"Everything alright, Tony?" Luca asked, pulling away from me and snapping me out of my hopeless romantic thoughts. I glanced over at Tony, who was biting his nails nervously and pacing up and down the span of his basement.

"It's just that-" he paused to bite his nails. "I guess, I guess I'm just nervous." Well, at least I was not alone there, but it pained me to see Tony feeling this way.

"Aren't we all?" I asked.

"I know that I am," Luca admitted.

"What if we get hate comments?"

The boys looked at me like I was crazy after I said that, and I wasn't sure why. It was a valid point, and it was a question that had popped into my mind more than once today.

"Why would you be afraid of that?" Luca asked.

This time, it was me who looked at him like he was crazy. "Aren't you scared of people judging you? I know that I am terrified of people talking bad about me, whether it be about my body, my voice, or just the way I look overall. I'm scared."

"No, you are not," Luca said under his breath, but I still heard him.

I wiped my head around and slammed my hand down on the coach, making the both of them jump.

"You think you know me?" I said in a whisper scream. "Do you honestly think you can tell me how I'm feeling at this moment?" I could feel the tears start to swell up again in my eyes, but I tried with all my might to hold them in. Their silence infuriated me even more as I continued, "Do you know how many second thoughts I've had? No, you don't. You don't know me." My eyes were locked on the two boys and my nostrils flared. Still, I got no response. "That's what I thought. I didn't even want to record with you guys. I hide, okay? Of course I'm scared about what people will think of our video."

It was true, my whole life I have developed the talent of hiding my real feelings. It all started in my junior high school, where people would constantly make fun of me for every little thing I said or did. It is one of my personality traits that prevents me from opening up to people, and I hate it. I've been hurt numerous times, and that's another reason why I bottle up all of my emotions, because I know that everytime I let people in, they just walk back out of my life. I also want to be strong for those around me, but this time, I chose not to hide from Luca and Tony because I felt that they should have full disclosure of how I'm feeling. Besides, I know that we all struggle with our own insecurities and that is why I was surprised at Luca's reaction.

Luca is a very mysterious person. He, like myself, is very closed off. I've seen how humble he is, and how he really does not enjoy the spotlight throughout the years I've known him. Luca loves to prove people wrong, however, and he has no shame in calling others out on their fraud. Sometimes I want to be like Luca, I want to acquire some of his qualities like his patience and kindness. I always knew that one can never really know a person fully, but I thought that Luca was more confident. I guess he could say the same about myself, but he carries himself with such confidence that it can be a tad intimidating.

Tony, on the other hand, is the more flamboyant kind. He truly did not care about judgement, or at least, that's what I had previously thought. I have seen him get up and sing karaoke at functions without regard to all the people laughing at the fact that he slurs his words whenever he's had a few drinks, and I admired that. Also, he is very smart and talented in the theatre department. He is the definition of a carefree person, and I love that about him.

I started to feel sick to my stomach at the fact that I unleashed some of my anger out on the boys. I felt bad that they now had to deal with my drama, and I never wanted to cause any problems. This always happens, I say some things that I regret and I look back and wish that I had bitten back my tongue. I should have been calm, after all, they didn't even have to entertain my dreams, and now we were staring at each other in silence. I could feel my jaw start to tremble and my face flushed.

"I'm so sorry." My words were quiet because I knew those three words would not change the fact that I just lashed out at the only two people who did not laugh at my dreams.

Chapter 8

Why did I have to create this awkward tension between the boys and myself? I constantly asked myself as I hurried over to the washroom. I could not bear the thought of them not wanting anything to do with me, so the tears started to flow down my face like a river. The scene of the previous events played in my mind like a mixtape on repeat. I shut the door, twisting the lock to ensure that nobody would walk in on me, and placed both of my hands on Tony's vanity. I took a deep breath as I stared at my reflection, my veins were popping out of my neck and my eyes were darting back and forth uncontrollably.

I had one job: don't do anything irresponsible and be polite. My dad's words rang in the back of my mind, and I was positive that my dad would be furious with me if he had to come pick me up right now, but there was no way I could stay here for the night. Tony and Luca's lack of response to my apology was a clear sign that they were hurt and wanted nothing to do with me or Insieme. My whole life I have been hurt, and so I try with all my heart to protect those I love, but now, I just hurt the two most amazing people I've ever met.

My tears started to stream down my face like a waterfall now; I was ugly crying. I was upset at Luca's obliviousness to my self consciousness. I was upset that I let my emotions get the best of me. Most of all, I was upset that I blew my shot with Insieme.

After twenty minutes, I had finally stopped crying, but only because there were no tears left to cry. I was debating whether or not I should go back out there and beg the boys for their forgiveness, but maybe I could spend the remainder of the evening locked away in Tony's beautiful bathroom.

"Giovanna?" A sweet voice that I did not recognize asked.

I knew it was not Luca or Tony because it was a woman who called out my name. I rolled up a few squares of toilet paper and dabbed at my eyes quickly as I opened the door. Standing in the doorway was a beautiful woman. I felt silly that I did not recognize her voice; it was Tony's mom. Her dark locks of wavy hair was in a loose, low- tied ponytail. Her eyes were filled with sympathy as she inched towards me. I opened my mouth to explain that everything was fine and that I'm sorry I woke her up, however she raised her hand to hush me.

"I know," she started, "the boys told me what happened."

Of course they did.

"Susana, I am so sorry, I didn't mean to wake you up," I apologized, noticing that Susana was in her baby blue nightgown

"There's no need to apologize," she assured me. "In fact, I am in agreement with you, and I told the boys that they are wrong."

"What do you mean?"

"It was foolish of them to think that you have all your feelings in check. I struggle with insecurities everyday, just like you, and I understand what you're going through."

"You do?" Susana probably thought I was stupid because I was barley saying anything, and when I did speak it was only to ask obvious questions.

She nodded, "I understand that you, like myself, sometimes struggle with your body image. Whether or not you're too round or too slim, but Gia, you're beautiful and it breaks my heart that you don't know that."

I stared at her silently as I wondered how she knew exactly what I was feeling. I have always felt alone and no one has ever understood what I was going through except my family and Mary.

"I also know that because you went to your grandmother's funeral when you were five years old is one of the reasons you are so closed-off. You were exposed to losing a loved one at an early age, and that's why you don't let people in. I also remember seeing you be strong for your younger cousins, and you have had my respect from that day on."

She struck a nerve. I really did not like to talk about my grandmother's passing with people. I remember that day vividly, but I don't remember seeing Susana there.

She must have seen the pained expression on my face because she quickly tried to recover, "I'm sorry, I didn't mean to bring up your grandmother."

"It's okay," I answered softly, the painful memories running through my mind.

"I want you to know that I haven't seen Tony this excited in a long time," she said, and I was happy that she was no longer talking about my grandmother. "Now he only talks about you and Luca, and sometimes I have to tell him to go do chores so he will stop talking."

I laughed as I pictured Tony rambling on about Insieme to his poor mother.

"The point is," she continued, "I was you to know that this, whatever this is, is not over. You don't have to be ashamed of who you are, and I know that the boys will support you no matter what. So, go join them." She motioned towards the door.

"Thank you, Susana." I looked at myself in the mirror one last time once Susana said goodnight to me. I took a deep breath and started to make my way over to the boys, but Luca and Tony were standing just two steps away from the door. I jumped up in shock and placed my hand on my heart as if that would somehow slow down it's rapid beat.

"How long have you been standing there?" I demanded.

"Long enough," Tony said as he handed me a beer as some sort of peace offering.

"Listen, Gia, you don't need to be sorry. I'm so sorry," Luca offered, tossing me the bottle opener.

"No, I should have handled the situation better," I said as I opened the cap and raised my bottle in the sky. The boys followed my footsteps and we clinked our bottles together before we took a big swig of our beers.

"I really do appreciate you guys, and I really am sorry," I expressed as we made our way over to the couch.

"Oh," Luca rolled his eyes, "you're that kind of drunk."

"I'm not even drunk!" I protested, swatting his arm playfully. The boys chuckled between the two of them, but it got quiet when Tony cleared his throat. I straightened my back as I waited for him to make his announcement.

"Let's promise not to fight again. Like a serious fight, you know?" He proposed.

"I promise," I stated.

"Yeah, me too, I promise," Luca said.

I could feel my cheeks start to go rosey as I took another drink from my beverage. I was surprised at how happy I was at this moment, given the fact that I can usually hold a grudge for at least a good two months. Maybe it was the alcohol, but there was not a bone in my body that was mad at either one of the boys.

"Hey!" I yelped as beer spilled down all over my chin and my outfit. Tony tipped my bottle high, and I could feel the bubble rushing up my nose.

The two of them were killing themselves with laughter. "Oh my goodness." I sprang up to my feet. The two of them were still busting a gut, even though my white romper was now stained a soft yellow. "My romper," I complained.

"Oh, Gia, just go upstairs and change into the sweatpants and shirt that I have laid out for you on the couch. Luca and I will get changed as well," he offered, trying to catch his breath from all the laughter, but him and Luca were still laughing as I made my way up the stairs.

I shook my head as I picked up the light grey sweatpants and matching sweatshirt and made my way to the nearest bathroom. I caught a short glimpse of myself in the mirror once I was changed into my new outfit. A sense of pride flushed down my spine as I looked at myself. I saw someone who used to be so worried about taking risks, and now here I was making videos of myself singing. I couldn't believe it.

"Took you long enough," Tony teased playfully once I returned to the basement. The two boys looked like a character straight out of *The Sopranos*. Both of them had on matching grey sweatpant shorts and a blank white wife beater with their gold chains dangling around their neck.

"I love your outfits," I commented, because I really did love their look.

The two of them blushed as they simultaneously rubbed the back of their neck with their right hand.

"Nice extra large crewneck, Gia," Luca scoffed as he went over to the coach where he laid down on his side.

"It's very fashionable," I responded, spreading my arms wide and doing a full 360 spin for the boys to admire my new look. The two of them found it hilarious, maybe it was the alcohol, but they were shaking uncontrollably with laughter. This time, I chimed in with a laughter of my own.

"We're like three bestfriends," Tony noted as he settled down next to Luca. His words sunk into my mind as I realized that I've known them for my entire life, but never considered them to be my best friends. I started to wonder what I would have done if I did not have that dream, would I just go on with my day to day life without even texting the boys? Even if our YouTube video does not work out, I'm forever grateful that the boys and I have been able to share a powerful bond.

Chapter 9

"Want another one, Giovanna?" Tony yelled as he opened the fridge door to get him and Luca another beer. I was already two beers deep and I was starting to feel a slight buzz. My father's words rang in the back of my mind, telling me to be responsible. There was no sense of peer pressure whatsoever, but it was really tempting to accept Tony's offer.

"Umm," I thought out loud, bringing my hand to my chin as I debated. "Sure."

Tony made his way over with three bottles of beer, and I could feel my heartbeat growing louder every time the bottle touched my lips.

Three beers quickly turned into six, and before I knew it, we were blasting music from Tony's speaker and screaming song lyrics at the top of our lungs. I could feel the bass guitar strums in my body and the room was spinning. The boys seemed to be just as drunk as me because they were stumbling over each other. I couldn't help but laugh and accept Tony's offer of another drink.

The three of us decided to turn on the television to find a movie we could all watch. Tony was searching through the guide, when he came across the movie *A Bronx Tale*.

"Can we watch that, please?" I asked, hoping that the boys would let me watch one of my favourite movies of all time. To my surprise, the boys did not argue with me and we ended up watching it.

A Bronx Tale has always been one of my favourites, mostly because I thought Calogero was very cute. I seemed to gravitate towards any kind of Robert DeNiro movie; he's a great actor. I loved the storyline behind the movie, *A Bronx Tale* is in my top five favourite movies of all time, and it's my comfort movie.

"Giovanna, how many times have you seen this movie?" Tony questioned, his eyes glued to the television, paying close attention to what was happening in the movie.

"Over five times, at least," I responded. I glanced over at Luca expecting to see him fixed on the movie, but his full attention was on his phone.

"Luca, come on, put the phone down," I said. "This is the best part of the movie!" I said as Calogero walked into the bar. Luca did not flinch a muscle as a perplexed expression came across his face. Tony peeked over at Luca as well, but rolled his eyes and put all of his attention back onto the movie. *That's Life* by Frank Sinatra started to play, my favourite Sinatra song, and I watched the screen intensely.

"Guys," Luca mumbled. I looked over to see his perplexed look had turned into a happier one.

"Not now, Luca." Tony raised his hand to shush him and turned up the volume on the movie.

Luca let out a sigh, which got my attention and I faced him because he usually only does that when something is very important.

"103 views."

My heart stopped, Tony turned down the TV. Butterflies came alive inside my stomach as I asked Luca to repeat what he just said.

"We have 103 views on our video already."

A flicker of hope went off in my heart. I knew that 103 views would not get us on the John Feton show, but that was pretty good considering that we just posted it about four hours ago. I was at a loss for words, I had so many questions but I did not know where to start. I tried to process that 103 people had viewed the three of us singing, and maybe they thought it was good or bad but I do not know.

"Any comments?" I asked, my legs bouncing rapidly.

"Two, one form a user named *Alex78*. He said 'Absolutely amazing.' Another one from *Sera05* saying 'I love this! Do more covers!'" Luca looked up from his phone with a smile spread across his face. We decided that it would be a good idea to celebrate by drinking just one more beverage.

Before I knew it, Tony was passed out on the couch and I was wrapped around Luca's waist. It must have been the alcohol in me because I was feeling confident, and that rarely happens. I was extremely dizzy, but somehow I still managed to have my lips tightly pressed against Luca's. Every rational thought had left my mind, and I knew that I should pull away from his grasp, but I couldn't. I knew that I would most likely regret this in the morning, but maybe we wouldn't remember it.

"Wow," he said, finally pulling away from me.

"I should go to bed," I whispered, and before he could say anything more I was already grabbing a blanket and making my way over to my designated couch. I couldn't even bring myself to look at him; I was so embarrassed. I knew that the sober me, the real me, would have been smarter, but all I knew is that I was liable to throw up any minute. Luca must have gotten the memo that I didn't want to see him anymore because it was dead silent in Tony's basement, except that Tony was snoring obnoxiously.

I tossed and turned, trying to find a comfortable position on Tony's couch, but I just couldn't allow myself to fall asleep. I was feeling happy, despite basically throwing myself at Luca earlier. I was so excited that our video already had 103 views, and I wondered if our views had gone up. I would check, but I had no idea where my phone was. I groaned as I flipped over to my left side, causing a ruffling noise to come from the other side of the room.

"Giovanna?" Luca asked in a tired, husky, voice. Shit. I woke him up and now I would actually have to talk to him because he was making his way over to me. I could hear him cursing quietly under his breath as he stumbled over every object that lied between his couch and mine in the pitch black room. "Why are you still awake?"

"I can't get comfortable," I whispered, sitting up to make room for Luca on Tony's small couch. He finally found my couch and sat directly next to me and I shared a piece of my blanket with myself.

"Same." It was incredibly awkward between the two of us, and I would rather be anywhere but here right now.

"I'm sorry," I said, even though I was not exactly sure what I was sorry for. I knew that I was ashamed of kissing him, or maybe he kissed me, I don't really know how it happened, but what did I have to be sorry for? I was three sheets to the wind.

"What are you sorry for? For encouraging us to form Insieme? You shouldn't be sorry, we have 103 views for crying out loud!"

"No, not that, but it really is amazing isn't it?" He nodded. "I guess I'm sorry for-" Before I could finish my thought, Luca had my face cupped in between both of his hands and his lips were on mine again. This time, I was more relaxed and dragged him down with me as I laid on my back so he was directly on top of me. As he pulled me closer, I allowed myself to stay tightly next to him, never wanting to let go.

Chapter 10

Click. "Awe! Look at how cute you guys are!" I slowly opened my eyes to the sound of Tony's camera and voice. He was standing in front of Luca and myself and flipped his phone around so we could see how the unwanted picture turned out. He captured the moment of me cradled in Luca's arms, my head buried into his chest. We both looked at peace in that photo.

"Can you send that to our group chat?" Luca asked as he rubbed his eyes. I sat up, but not for long, immediately bolting for the bathroom. I rushed into the bathroom and I instantly dropped to my knees in front of the toilet, letting out all of the alcohol I had consumed last night. I could hear the boys rush to my side, Luca quickly pulling my hair away from my face and Tony rubbing my back.

"I'm going to get her some water and medicine," Tony said to Luca.

"You'll be alright," Luca hushed to me as I had my head buried in the toilet bowl. There was no sign of my vomit lighting up any time soon. I could feel my guts churning and my back aching with every hurl I gave up.

"Take this," Tony instructed, handing me a glass of water and two white pills that I assume are Advil.

"Thank you," I said weakly, my voice didn't sound like normal. I tried to take the glass from Tony, but I nearly dropped it. I guess my voice was not the only thing that was weak this morning. Tony quickly saved the cup from shattering into a million pieces on the floor and Luca tipped my head back so Tony could place the pills in my mouth. Luca tied my hair into a messy ponytail once I finally managed to swallow the pills.

"Do you want us to give you some space?" Luca asked softly.

"Could you-" My head was buried yet again in the toilet before I could finish my sentence, and the boys sighed as they continued to rub my back and hold back loose hair strands. I felt awful. The boys seemed completely fine, no sight of a hangover whatsoever, but that was clearly not the case for me.

"Take your time, your dad isn't coming to pick you up until 7:00 pm," Tony said. "Do you remember anything from last night?"

"No," I lied. Luca just softly stroked my forehead with a damp cloth, and I took that as a sign that he didn't want to talk about our kiss either. It wasn't that Luca was a bad guy, he was so sweet, but a relationship would just complicate things. If we get together and then end up having to break up, that would be so bad for Insieme, and I can't let that happen.

"Do you remember how many views we have on our video?"

"I remember you telling me that we have just over 100 views, but everything else after that I don't remember." Despite feeling absolutely terrible this morning, I was still overwhelmed with emotions over the outcome of our video.

"Do you think you'll be able to go back to the couch?" I nodded and the boys slowly helped me get to my feet and guided me over to the couch.

"Someone can't hold down their alcohol," Luca said.

"Shut up," I laughed, resting my head against the cushion.

Usually, I wanted to be in the comfort of my own home the mornings of sleepovers; unless, of course, I slept over at Mary's. However, I did not want to go home on this bright sunny day. I wanted to stay with the boys and keep making videos, keep sharing our hopes, and maybe even write our own songs. Tony scurried upstairs to ask Susana for some old clothes I could borrow today, leaving Luca and I alone.

"Do you seriously not remember anything that happened last night?" Luca asked in a serious tone.

"I don't," I assured him. "Do you?"

"Yeah, I remember everything, I'm not a light weight like you," he teased. "So you don't remember the kiss?" Shoot. Why did he have to bring this up? What was I supposed to say?

"Oh, that's right, I remember now."

Tony ran down the stairs with a pair of mom jeans and a graphic T-shirt.

"Your mother has great style!" I complimented as I snached the clothes from his hands and rushed back into the washroom.

I got out of the grey sweatpants and crewneck and folded them nicely together. I slipped on the light wash blue jeans and tucked in

Susana's *Purple Rain* shirt into them. I looked at myself in the mirror, Susana's jeans hugging my body perfectly. The black T-shirt with purple print on it was on the baggier side, but it added to the vintage look. I quickly tied my hair into a high ponytail, allowing two strands of curls to fall carelessly down my face. I looked as though I was taken right out of a 1980's movie set.

I made my way over to the boys and set down the sweatpants.

"Oh, she's a stunner," Tony commented as he stared at me. I could feel my face flush into a deep red blush, and I did not know what to say. I let out a nervous laugh as I tucked one of my curls behind my ear.

"Don't look at me like that," I scolded, clearing my throat in embarrassment. I knew I looked good, but I just do not know how to take compliments.

"You look amazing," Luca added, making my already reddened cheeks heat up even more.

"Breakfast?" I asked, wanting to change the subject.

"Right this way." Tony ushered, making his way up the stairs.

"I knew you would love the outfit!" Susana gasped as she caught sight of me upstairs.

"It's so cute!" I agreed as I sat down at the table. I was surprised at how well I could hide my pounding headache and churning guts, but hopefully food will help.

Susana served us homemade waffles with fresh blueberries and raspberries on top. I poured some syrup and waited patiently for Tony and Luca to come sit down. It was tradition in my family to wait until everyone was sitting at the table before anyone started to eat. Even if I was starving, I was trained to wait politely for the others.

Finally, Luca and Tony came to the table in a fresh outfit, both of them in a pair of jeans and a golf shirt. Their outfit gave me a great idea.

"We should go golfing soon." I proposed as I dug into my fluffy waffles.

"That was random," Luca said, letting out a groan as he sat down at the table. "I hate golf."

"Why?" Tony and I asked at the same time.

"Because it's boring and long. Who would ever in the right mind spend hours in the blistering sun just to hit a tiny white ball."

"Well, we could just do a nine whole course," I suggested. "Come on, it will be so fun!"

Luca shook his head in protest, "No. I refuse."

"Don't be a jerk," Tony piped in. "It's worth a shot, and besides, I'm not that good at golf but I'll still go. We can all just laugh at each other, except Gia, she's a professional golfer." I laughed at his statement; I was anything but that.

One time, my dad took me golfing with him and it was the first stroke. My dad, patient as always, taught me proper form, so I was feeling pretty confident in the Tee Box. I stepped up to swing my club and hit the ball, however; the club flew out of my hands when I followed through and hit my dad directly on his shoulder. Of course, we had a good laugh about it, but he still brings it up all the time. It's one of those stories that my dad refuses to let go.

"Fine, but don't expect me to be exactly thrilled to be out in the course," Luca pouted.

The three of us finished breakfast, and Tony made the suggestion of going for a walk. I put all my dishes in the dishwasher and thanked Susana, and made my way over to my shoes.

"Wait a second, Giovanna." Susana stopped me and grabbed my arm. I gave her a puzzled look and she started to speak in a hushed voice, "I saw the video." My heart sped up, waiting for her to elaborate.

"Oh, yeah?" I said awkwardly, trying to get Susana to loosen her grip on my right arm.

"Yeah, and I just wanted to tell you that it sounded amazing. You kids have no idea how proud I am, and I want you to know that after I finish cleaning up I will promote the video as well. You guys sound natural together, and I admire that. I admire you the most, though." My facial expression must have given away my concerned feelings for Tony because Susana quickly back peddled, "Of course, I'm proud of Tony. He's my son. I'll always be proud of him. However, I'm proud of you because I know the struggles you have gone through." I glanced quickly at the floor, worried that I might burst into tears if I kept up the eye contact.

"I hate to keep bringing up your grandmother," *I hate it too*, I thought, "but I just know she would be so proud." I knew my Nonna would be proud, and that's why tears started to trickle down my cheeks. "I'm 45 years old, but I've been learning so much from you in a short amount of time. I want to be as strong as you." Although her words were kind, I was still thinking about my grandmother. I tried to say thank you, but I made no sound. My throat was tight and my hands were shaking, and I looked into Susana's eyes hoping she would understand how much I appreciated her words. She gave me a quiet nod and nudged me towards the door where I saw Luca and Tony waiting for me. I glanced back at Susana with a tired smile and went on my way.

"You alright?" Tony asked, noticing my tear stained cheeks.

"Yeah, don't worry about it," I said as I started to sing *Here Comes The Sun* by The Beatles.

"I didn't know you liked The Beatles," Luca commented, grabbing hold of my hand.

"Everyone likes The Beatles." I tensed up immediately and quickly removed my hand from his grip. This couldn't happen. I wouldn't allow it.

We continued to make our way through Tony's neighbourhood, and I noticed how slow of a walker I am with my short legs. I could barely keep up with the boys and I would often have to call out for them and ask them to wait for me or slow down.

"Let's stop by my house," Luca suggested as we rounded the corner. Tony and Luca live very close together, and I am so jealous of that.I had seen Luca's parents plenty of times, and I absolutely loved his dad. I wondered if they knew about the trio we formed, or if they were still waiting for university football teams to scout Luca.

Luca led the way to a massive grey house with jet black trim. A basketball hoop sat at the base of their driveway and I suggested that we should play after we talk to his parents. He knocked on the door and the three of us stepped back a few steps as we waited for his parents to open up. I had seen Luca's parents plenty of times, and I absolutely loved his dad. I wondered if they knew about the trio we formed, or if they were still waiting for university football teams to scout Luca.

"Oh! What a pleasant surprise!" Anna claimed shockingly as she opened the door to let us in. I stepped inside the house where I was greeted by Luca's tiny dog, Marco. I gently stroked Marco's fur as I waited to give Anna a hug.

"How are you, Giovanna?" She asked as she pulled me in for a tight hug.

"I'm great, how are you?"

"Oh, I'm just fantastic." Anna puckered her lips together, finally losing her grip on me. I let out a nervous laugh as I tried to untangle myself from her embrace.

"Look who the cat dragged in," Giancarlo stated as he walked towards me with open arms. He swooped me into his large body and hugged me so tight I could not breath, bringing back the dizzy feeling I had felt when I first woke up.

"Well, maybe if you had my family over for dinner sometime," I fired back jokingly at Luca's dad.

My family had them over for dinner one night, about two years ago now, and we have not been invited to their house once. We keep waiting, but we know it will never happen. The only time I see Luca or his family is at big Italian banquets, and most of the time I'm performing so I rarely see them. However, I had a soft spot for Giancarlo because he protected me from this guy I almost dated.

"Oh, give me a break," he pleaded as I let out a genuine laugh.

"Dad, why don't we have them over for dinner?" Luca asked, clearly confused.

"Yeah, Gian, why don't you have us over for dinner?" I questioned as I crossed my arms and raised my eyebrows jokingly.

"Because-" he started.

"Because my mom's cooking was too good and he knows he can't top it," I finished for him as I nudged his shoulder.

"Oh my gosh," Giancarlo rolled his eyes as he laughed.

"Well, it's true," I explained looking over at Tony who was in deep conversation with Anna.

"Tony," I called, making Tony snap his head towards me, "you've had my mom's cooking before.

It's the best right?" He shot me a look to say *Thank you for saving me* and made his way over to the three of us.

"The greatest," he agreed, and I gave Giancarlo and Luca a triumphant look.

"My cooking is good, too," Anna piped up. I gave Tony a look and scoffed at his expression as he braced himself because he knew what was coming.

"Well, I wouldn't know, Anna. I've never had your cooking." Everyone burst into laughter, except for Anna. She seemed a bit hurt so I had to quickly recover, "I'm only messing with you."

She lightened up and ushered us to the table.

"I take it Vince is still out in British Columbia for university?" I asked, noticing that Luca's older brother was not home.

"You don't need Vince when you have me," Lorenzo announced, grinning from ear to ear.

Lorenzo is Luca's younger brother, and him and I would always go back and forth with corny jokes.

"Oh, lucky me," I rolled my eyes, but Lorenzo was already sprinting into my lap where he draped one arm around my neck and twisted sideways himself so he could see Luca.

"Where have you been?" He asked.

"At Tony's," Luca responded as he brought out his phone. "Take a look at this, buddy." He gave his brother his phone that was already opened up to our YouTube video.

"That's you guys!" He noted as he gazed up at me. I nodded and pressed the play button for him, noticing that our views were up to 237 and we now had 84 comments. A rush of excitement surged through me and I almost started to bounce my leg, but I remembered that Lorenzo was still sitting on my lap.

I listened carefully to how wonderful we sounded, and I noticed that Lorenzo's face was lit up. Gian craned his neck so he could watch the video as well, and Anna placed the glasses of lemonade down for all of us and watched silently, too. The video finished and I could see how proud his parents were of Luca, of all of us.

"Gia carried," Lorenzo announced as he took a big chug of lemonade.

"No, all of us sounded amazing," I assured him and he shrugged as he aggressively drank from the glass.

"Wow, buddy, have you not had a drink in three days?" Luca teased as he placed his phone back in his pocket.

"I loved it," Giancarlo commented.

"It was like listening to the angels in Heaven," Anna said, which was an exaggeration, but we all thanked them.

"So you all slept over at Tony's then?" Giancarlo asked.

"Yeah, look at this." Tony laughed as he pulled out his phone and showed the selfie with the three of us smiling brightly, and then the picture of myself snuggled into Luca.

"You guys are so cute," Anna commented. Luca and I made eye contact for a split second before I quickly looked away. "Why don't you guys all come for dinner at 6 tonight then?" I wondered if she genuinely wanted me to be there, or if she felt bad about never having us over.

"Like, just us, or our whole family?" Tony asked, reading my mind.

"The whole family!" She offered, looking directly at me.

"Um, you should call my parents or else they won't believe me," I joked, looking at Giancarlo who scoffed and shook his head.

"Will do," he said as he walked over to his phone and started calling my houseline.

"Gia, I hope you know you're beautiful. Have you ever been told?" Lorenzo asked me out of the blue as he stared at me with his big eyes.

"Thank you," I gushed as he squeezed the back of my neck tightly. "I'll admit, I have been told, but when it comes from you, it's the best."

He giggled and blushed, "Wanna play with me?"

"No, Lorenzo," Luca protested, but I nodded my head and suggested basketball, trying my hardest to hide my hangover.
The two of us got up, and I thanked Anna for the lemonade and followed quickly after Lorenzo.

"I didn't know my brother could sing," he admitted when we got outside.

"He's amazing isn't he."

"Yeah, you know, G, I always wondered if he was okay. Sometimes he would be completely silent after one of his football games, even if he played amazing. I never asked him what was wrong because I did not want to bother him, but one day he opened up to me when I walked in on him crying in his room."

"Are you sure you're allowed to tell me this story?"

"Yeah, anway," he continued, "I've never seen him genuinely happy. In that video, he looks content. He looks like he finally found a purpose, I guess. You're good for him. A good influence."

I was taken aback by his kind words, but I also wondered how I could help Luca. I wanted to be a rock for him; someone who he could always lean on. I wanted to say thank you to Lorenzo, but Tony and Luca came outside and insisted that we all couple up and play a full game of basketball.

Before I could question Lorenzo further without being too obvious about how much I cared about Luca, we were playing basketball. I wanted to

ask Lorenzo why Luca doubts his worth so much,
and I wanted to know how I could help him.

Chapter 11

"30-15," Luca declared. I, unfortunately, got paired up with Tony. Tony was not the best player, as a matter of fact, I had scored all of our 15 points. I was surprisingly shocked at how good Lorenzo was considering he was younger than all of us. Luca, was just lucky that Tony was so bad, or else he would get carried by his younger brother.

We finally finished the match and headed on inside where we announced we were heading back to Tony's place.

"Oh, Gia," Giancarlo stopped me. "I spoke to your mom, and your family is coming over for dinner tonight."

"Wake me up from this dream," I teased, nudging him on the shoulder. He shook his head and hugged me goodbye. Everyone was standing by the door, and just when I was about to leave Lorenzo stopped me.

"I can't wait for dinner tonight. I miss you already." He hugged me closely, and joy rushed inside me.

"Don't worry, I'll be back in a few hours," I assured him as I caught up to the boys.

"My brother loves you," Luca commented when we were no longer near his house.

"I couldn't tell," Tony scoffed, jealousy wrapped all over his comment. I pushed Tony gently, but he decided to be dramatic and flop onto the sidewalk.

"No wonder your favourite subject is drama," I mocked as I helped him to his feet, and we continued to walk in silence the rest of the way back.

"Did anyone else notice that our views went up?" Tony asked as soon as we walked into his house.

"That's pretty amazing," Luca said, slipping his hand around my waist as he brushed past me. I averted my eyes to the ground and remained silent. We followed Tony downstairs where he gave us each a Pepsi. The three of us played Madden as I forced the boys to listen to my playlist that was filled with One Direction songs. Once my playlist was over, Susana called Tony upstairs.

"So are you just going to ignore me now?" Luca asked, inching closer towards me.

"I'm not ignoring you," I defended.

"You've barely said anything to me and you can't even look me in the eyes."

"I'm hungover," I said. "Every little thing that I do makes my head pound and makes me nauseous."

"So when my mom said that we're cute and you refused to look at me, that was because you were nauseous?"

"What was I supposed to do?" I was surprised at how calm I was remaining.

"You could at least give me a chance," he whispered. "It was just one kiss, and I'm not really sure why you regret it so much."

"I don't regret it." I did. Very much.

He scoffed, reading right through my lie, "I don't understand. Was I bad or something?"

"I just don't think the two of us should get involved with each other; it'll complicate things."

"Just give me a shot," he pleaded. "I've given you no reason not to trust me." That was true, but I still had a gut feeling that this would ruin everything, especially with our views going up.

"I can't," I whispered. "We can't."

"Guys, come upstairs, we're heading to Luca's house now," Tony called out. I sighed as I got up, and I noticed that Luca was wiping a single teardrop from his eye. Oh boy.

Chapter 12

"Hello everyone," I announced as I walked over to my parents and brother.

"How was your night?" My mom pressed immediately. My mom has a habit of interrogating my brother or myself everytime we go out. She would always ask about what we did or who was there or what we talked about. Of course, I would usually give her a brief summary of the night before, but this time, Tony decided to go into detail about our night.

"Oh, it was so fun! It all started when Gia told us about her dream the other day."

"What dream?" My mother interrupted as she stared at me. I shot Tony a look before I glanced over at dad, who I thought would have filled her in by now, but he just simply shrugged. *Thanks for your help, dad.*

"Um... I had a dream the other night, and the boys were in it," I started. "You see, we were on the John Feton show and we were in a trio called Insieme."

"*Insieme?*" She wondered. "Like the song?"

"Yes, like the song. Anyway, long story short, we were famous and I told the boys about my dream. We agreed that we would release a YouTube video of the three of us singing together to see if we could possibly make my dream come true." I let out a big breath, my heart racing as my mother remained painfully silent.

"As I was saying," Tony continued, oblivious of the sudden tension between my mother and myself. "We first sang karaoke individually, and then decided to sing Story Of My Life for our YouTube video."

"You left out the part where I destroyed you in Madden," I added, hoping my mother would join in the laughter with everyone else, but she remained silent with a cold look on her face. At this point, I could hear the rapid thumping of my heartbeat in my head, and I wanted to escape my mother's glare. I wondered why she was not being as supportive as dad. I knew that as soon as we returned to my house she would try and talk me out of this, and I could feel myself thinking up fake scenarios of my mother yelling at me later.

"Why didn't you tell me?" My mom asked with a hint of pain in her tone.

"I knew you would laugh," I admitted. I scratched the back of my now sweaty neck nervously as every single set of eyes in the room were glued to me.

"Why would I laugh?" Her nostrils flared out with every word she spoke, and her face was becoming a dark shade of red.

"I don't know," I shrugged innocently. I just didn't want to bother you."

"You should have told me."

Her lack of enthusiasm made me want to cry and scream at the same time. How come she could not be understanding? At the same time, I knew she was right, I should have told her. I've always felt embarrassed to tell my dreams to my mother, and I'm not sure why because my whole life she has been my number one fan.

"I saw the video," My brother piped up. Antonio always knew when to interject into my mother and I's conversations. "I was very impressed, but I was even more impressed with how much love you guys are receiving from it."

"I want to see it," My dad pleaded, my mother said nothing but I saw she was clearly intrigued. Soon enough, Luca was pulling up his phone and showed the video to my parents. It seemed as though everyone else in the room had already seen it, and I was quite honestly hurt that my parents had not seen it yet. It made me feel as though my parents were too busy to notice this new path that I so desperately wanted to take, and everyone else seemed to already be on board with our new train of thought.

When the video was over I saw that both my parents were wearing a proud smile. I also saw my mom wipe away some tears that had escaped her eyes. Despite my feelings of hurt because they had not viewed the video, I was over the moon that they thoroughly enjoyed our cover.

"Time for dinner!" Anna announced as she drained the steaming hot pasta. I went into the kitchen to join the rest of the ladies.

"I'm sorry, Mamma," I said sheepishly as I pulled her aside. "I should have told you."

"It's okay, I'm sorry if I did anything to make you feel like you could not come talk to me. I just wish I would have recognized your talent earlier," she stated, and I wanted to assure her that she did nothing wrong, but she gave me a quick hug before I had the chance and she insisted that I help Anna serve the food.

I brought many bowls of piping hot pasta to the boys sitting at the dinner table and I intentionally gave Lorenzo an extra spoonful of pasta. Lorenzo insisted that he sat next to me, and the whole time he kept making silly faces whenever I looked at him.

"Well, I have to tell you a funny story about this morning," Giancarlo said, turning towards my parents as he explained how I joked about never being over for dinner.

"It's true!" I protested as I laughed at Lorenzo's attempt at a sassy face.

As everyone finished up the meal, I started to help clear out the plates. I excused myself to the washroom and left the room quietly.

See how natural this feels? It feels like we're all family. I thought as I stared myself down in the mirror. My ponytail was coming undone, but my curls were still coiled tightly. I attempted to make another knot with my scrunchie so my long ponytail would stay in place. I needed a break from a crowd every now and then, and I definitely needed a break to collect my thoughts about what is happening between me and the boys.

I started to wonder how many views and comments we have on our video now, and I wanted to know why everyone liked it. I knew that we sounded good together. I longed for that feeling of walking onto any stage and hearing the crowd roar our names. I want to be known in life; I do not want to just live a boring life. I want to make music that inspires people, just like how music inspires me. I want people to feel something whenever they hear the three of us sing, and I want to be a role model to society. I know that a single YouTube video probably won't affect that many people's hearts and minds, but I want to try. I believe that I had that dream on purpose, and I believe that it will work out.

I took one last glance at myself before I made my way out. As I walked back to the crowd, I saw that they were in a heated game of Rummoli, and I quickly joined Tony and Luca on the couch and watched our parents play. After a long hour of hearing them scream at each other and get competitive, I realized that I wanted to go home. Not that I don't love the boys, but I needed some sleep. My parents must have read my mind because they stated that they were tired and that we should get going.

I made my way around the room, hugging and kissing everyone two times on the cheek before moving onto the next person. When I came to Lorenzo he seemed sad, and then he started to speak. "Don't leave me all alone." I did not know what to say, and I stared at him blankly for what felt like five minutes. Fortunately, Luca chimed in, "Oh, don't worry, Enzo. We'll be seeing Gia more often now because she will be spending a lot more time with me and Tony, so I'm sure you'll see her around." Once again, I broke Luca and I's eye contact.

I hugged Lorenzo goodbye and Luca pulled Tony and myself aside.

"Let's all relax tomorrow, but why don't we hang out... What day is it today?" he asked.

"Sunday," Tony replied.

"Let's hangout Tuesday then."

"I'm instructing Tuesday night, what about Wednesday?" I suggested.

"Wednesday works for me," Tony shared, and Luca said it will work as well.

"Love you guys," Luca said. I murmured the words back under my breath and made my way to my car, a million thoughts and doubts filling my mind.

Chapter 13

"He did what?" Mary blurted, making me
instantly turn down the volume on my phone. My
hangover seemed to have subsided when I woke
up, and I went through the remainder of Monday
morning alright, so I decided to facetime my best
friend.

"I don't really remember who leaned in first,
but all I know is that we kissed," I responded.

"How was he!"

"I don't know," I protested. "He was my first
kiss."

"And you don't remember it? That's sad,"
she said. "Why did you guys drink so much?"

"I guess we just wanted to celebrate our
video getting 100 views within the first few hours of
posting it."

"What video?"

"Insieme's video," I said, as if she should
already know this, but then I realised that I never
actually told Mary what Insieme even is. "Sorry, I
should have told you. Basically, Tony, Luca, and
myself decided to form a singing trio after the
dream I had about being famous on the John Feton

show. We decided that if I had a dream about the three of us being famous together, it would be worth a shot to try and make that dream come true. The other night posted a video of us covering *Story Of My Life by* One Direction."

"I'm going to go watch it right now, partially because you are my best friend, but mostly because I love that song," she laughed, but she muted herself and did exactly what she said she would. A few minutes later she returned. "I love it! I love it so much! You guys sound so good together."

"Thank you," I said, letting out a nervous laugh because I simply did not know how to take a compliment.

"I'm going to repost the link on my instagram story, so even more people can see it," Mary said quickly because she was clearly excited.

"You're the best," I chuckled.

"Okay, as much as I love this video," she began, "I need to know what's going on between you and Luca. Are your parents home?"

"No."

"Good. So, what's going on between you two, and what about Danny?" She asked eagerly.

"I don't want anything to happen between Luca and myself because that will just complicate things with Insieme." I gave her the same reason I had mentally given myself.

"And Danny?" She pressed.

"I don't know, Mar. I've liked him ever since science class started, but I don't think he likes me back. I am almost ninety-nine percent certain that he just sees me as a friend."

"Well, maybe if you guys talked about something other than sports," she said.

"Sports is the only thing that I can talk about without getting all tongue-tied," I explained.

"This is true." We both laughed because we knew that I was completely incapable of holding a regular conversation if it didn't involve sports.

"I mean, is Luca a bad guy? No, but I've just never thought about him as more than a brother," I continued. "On the other hand, Danny and I will probably go nowhere together."

"Sorry, why don't you want to date Luca? He seems pretty into you, why don't you give him a chance?"

I sighed, "It's just that with everything going on right now I don't think it's a good idea to complicate things."

"Fair enough, but then can you and Danny get together, please? I've been waiting for you guys to get together for, like, ever."

"I'll try," I said, "but I can't make any promises. Anway, are you ready for dance class tomorrow?"

"Always," she confirmed. "I need to go help my mother with dinner, see you tomorrow."

"Bye, I love you."

"Love you too." And with that I was left all alone in my house with nobody to talk to. I could have responded to all my unopened messages, but I didn't want to.

I cooked a small pot of pasta for Antonio and myself, once I got a text from my parents saying that they won't be home until late this evening.

"How are you?" my brother asked once he finished his food.

"I'm good, how are you?"

"No," he got serious all of a sudden, "how are you really doing?"

"I'm doing good," I lied.

"No you're not. This whole singing thing, where did this come from?" I knew that he meant well, but his words came out a bit bitter.

"I told you, I had a dream."

"I just want to know if you're doing okay mentally," he said gently. "I just worry about you sometimes."

"There's no need," I assured him.

My brother was painfully silent before he spoke, "I heard your video, I know you guys will make it. I just, I guess I've just heard stories of people forgetting their families once they get famous." I could see the worry in his eyes, and it broke my heart.

"Antonio, don't even think about that right now. I assure you that I won't forget about you or anyone else. You and I have been best friends since I came out of our mother's womb. When I'm feeling lost, who do I turn to for advice?"

He shot his eyes down and mumbled, "Me."

"That's right," I nodded. "Now, what makes you think I'll forget you, my own brother. We've been through so much together, and I can assure you that if, by some miraculous miracle, Insieme takes off, I won't forget you. I promise." It boggles my mind that my brother, my own blood, would think that I would disregard him if I make it in the big leagues.

"I'm sorry if I made it sound like I don't want you to find success," he apologized as he hung his head down. "I just worry about you, that's all."

"There's nothing to worry about. I'm doing this for you and our parents, not for me. I want to make you guys proud," I admitted.

"Everything you do makes us proud. I don't think you understand how proud dad was when he found out you are instructing dance this year, and how proud mom is whenever you perform at your dance recitals. They love you, and I love you."

"I love you." And with that my brother left me all alone.

After I finished working out and showering, it was pitch black in my house, only the faint glow of my desk lamp lit up my room. I was quietly reading my self-development book, trying to improve my confidence. I always found interest in those books, and people at school like to make fun of me for always reading instead of texting them back, but I don't really care. Unfortunately, my reading session was cut short by my phone buzzing obnoxiously on the corner of my desk. I picked it up and saw Luca's name sprawled across the screen and let out a loud groan.

"Hey," I said reluctantly. It's not that I had anything against Luca, I just found it weird that he would be FaceTiming me late at night. I guess I didn't find it weird a few days ago, but everything seemed to have changed after the kiss.

"Hi," he smiled. "Did I wake you up?"

"No, I was just reading," I answered.

"Oh nice, what are you reading?"

"*The 7 Habits of Highly Effective People.*" Why did he care what book I was reading? Why was this awkward?

"Is it good?"

"I guess," I sighed. "Is there something you need from me?" My question sounded more impatient than I had intended and I quickly apologized.

"It's alright," he said. "I just couldn't sleep."

"Why not?"

He threw his head back as he answered, "I just can't stop thinking about Insieme."

"We should add Tony to the call then," I proposed, hoping that Tony would ease up the awkwardness.

"Are you sure that everything is good between us?" He asked, and I was very tempted to hang up on him to avoid this conversation.

"I don't really know what you're expecting me to say," I said. "I've already expressed that I would not have kissed you if I was sober."

"But we did," he said impatiently. "You can't just avoid me forever."

"How am I avoiding you? I'm still singing with you and Tony, I'm still going to your house for dinner, and I'm still picking up your FaceTime calls." I was genuinely confused.

"Whenever someone brings up the idea of us being together, you automatically look down and can't even look at me. Is there something wrong with me, Giovanna? Am I that bad of a guy? Do you think I'm not good enough for you?" His voice quavered, and my eyes filled with empathy. I hated seeing him like this, despite the fact that I was the one causing him to question his worth.

"Luca, you are a great guy, and any girl would be lucky to be with you," I started. "I just feel as though we are more like brother and sister, and it would just be too awkward."

"That's bullshit and you know it. I'm not stupid."

"It's not," I defended. "It's just how I feel."

"I'm sorry, it's just that there's so much going on right now and I guess I'm just stressed."

I chuckled, "Me too."

"I'll let you get some sleep and I won't bother you anymore," he whispered, already climbing into his bed.

"You're never a bother," I assured him. "Goodnight."

"Is it still weird to say that I love you? I just say it to everyone because we never really know if we will see each other again."

"I love you, Luca," I laughed and hung up the call.

I layed wide awake on my back, looking up at my ceiling. I was debating what to do with Luca. He was a great guy, but my gut was just telling me not to get involved. If there is one thing that I've learned from that past is that my gut is always right.

All my thoughts about Luca circled back to Insieme, and led me to pull up the video on my phone. I noticed that we had 468 views now and a lot more comments than before. It was overwhelming. The thought of over 400 people seeing our video and actually hearing the three of us sing.

I scrolled through the comments and smiled at all the encouragement. However, my smile was quickly wiped off my face when I saw a comment that read.

Sonia05: Why is everyone lying to them in the comment section? They are clearly out of tune, especially the girl, and they don't even sound good together. Delete this before it's too late.

What. Obviously, I wasn't expecting every single person to like our video, but it still hurt. It hurt even more because when I clicked on the user's profile I saw a bunch of school blogs uploaded to their page, and I immediately recognized Sonia's face. I cursed under my breath. I have been able to put up with her at school, but now she just touched the boys, and I didn't like that at all. I wondered how the boys would react to this, but I didn't wonder for long because our group chat was already aware.

Tony: Did you guys see the new comment?

Luca: What's up with that?

Tony: Why do people feel the need to be mean?

Luca: My fear came true.

Tony: Maybe we should delete the video.

Oh, no. There was no way I was going to allow the boys to delete the video over one silly little comment.

Me: Don't delete it. I know who she is, she goes to my school, I'll explain on Wednesday.

I heard my phone buzz again, but I didn't bother reading whatever the boys had to say. I was extremely tired and I couldn't believe that they wanted to delete the video over one hate comment.

I thought they knew that this was inevitable to happen, and it just so happened to be somebody I knew. Perhaps I would have been more sad if it was stranger, but I knew that this was just Sonia's insecurities talking. She always has something bad to say about me, and I hate myself for being a coward around her. It didn't even cross my mind that she would see the video, it didn't even cross my mind that hundreds of people would see it. I thought we would only get three views, and those viewers would only be our family, but I was wrong.

Eventually, I allowed my brain to shut off and I was able to fall asleep.

"Ready to go?" My mom asked me. I was certainly not ready, I was still in my leggings and sports bra with all of my shirts that I owned sprawled on the floor. I couldn't find my dance shirt and I had been searching forever, and now I would be late.

"Have you seen my dance shirt?" I yelled from my room, and then I heard my mom climbing up the stairs moments after.

She gasped at the sight of my room. "It's right here." She picked up the shirt off of my desk chair and shot me a look. I quickly threw the shirt over my head and dashed out the door, holding my runners and water bottle in my hand.

My mom sped the whole way there, but she also talked my ear off the entire drive as well. She went on and on about what customers she had to deal with, and she talked about Insieme and how she noticed that our views kept going up, and she also talked about how happy she is that I am instructing. I've never heard my mom talk this much, and it was kind of worrisome, but I didn't ask her because she never gave me the chance to speak.

"Bye, I love you," she said, and before I could say anything, she zoomed off onto the bustling street.

I walked up the stairs into a narrow hallway that led to our studio. Mary had not yet arrived, so I decided to run through the steps of our new dance.

The dance studio was my happy place- it was like an escape- and I always enjoyed my time there. I had no worries when I was dancing, and the only thing I would think about is the next dance step I needed to take.

I decided to join the dance group for my grandmothers. I lost them at a young age and I wanted to make them proud, and embrace their culture. I wanted to feel connected to them in a sense. I knew that they would have loved to see me dance and instruct little girls and perform on big stages. I always wanted to find new friends, and I ended up meeting Mary.

We connected instantly, we were genuinely comfortable with each other. There were no secrets between us, and neither of us pushed each other to tell one another about every single detail of our lives. We respect each other's boundaries and work very well together. We are both easygoing, but have a sense of direction at the same time.

Mary finally walked into the studio just ten minutes before our students would begin to arrive with an iced coffee for herself and a lemonade for me.

"Here you go, sorry there was a lineup at Tim Hortons," she apologized.

"Thank you!" I responded, shocked that she would think to stop for me.

I hate coffee, and I did not understand how she could drink iced coffee on a daily basis. I found it too bitter, even with extra sugar and creamer. I know that lemonade is typically for younger children, but it was my go-to order.

Mary and I talked about our day and what we wanted to do for today's class. We ran through our new dance we created to make sure that all of the counts were correct. Soon enough, our first student walked in.

"Hi, Miss Mary! Hi, Miss Giovanna!" One of our students said, prancing into the studio.

The rest of our dancers trickled in and we began class. We laughed and joked the whole class. Mary and I made a promise to each other that we would never be hard on the girls. We wanted to be welcoming and make them feel safe and comfortable. We wanted them to love being part of the Folk Dancers, and we wanted them to have fun.

Our class only lasted an hour and fifteen minutes before we said goodbye to our class. The girl's parents started to make their way into the parking lot, and we guided them to their cars. When all the girls had left safely, Mary and I headed back inside.

"That went well," I stated.

"It always does," Mary responded with a proud smile.

"So, I'm seeing Tony and Luca tomorrow," I began. "I don't quite know what to expect tomorrow, but I'm kind of nervous."

"How come?" She asked as she started to play *cardigan* by Taylor Swift, one of our favourite songs.

"I don't know," I shrugged. "I guess I'm just worried that they'll back out of the plan. They're already considering deleting the video."

"Giovanna, look at this." She pulled up my instagram feed and showed the pictures I had just posted with Tony and Luca. "They care about you! There's no need to worry, and besides, I'm sure they want this just as bad as you do," she assured me.

She was right, the boys had been so open with me, and I even cried in front of them.

"You're right," I agreed. "Should we post another YouTube video?"

"Maybe see what the boys want, but I would love to see another video posted."

We talked for about another hour about school, what song Insieme should sing next, and dance. We were silenced when we heard a faint knock on the door.

"Come in?" I hesitated. Our mother's walked in with their heads held high.

"Hello, ladies!" My mother stated as the two of them greeted us both with hugs.

"Maria! I have not seen you in forever, how are you?" I asked.

"It's been too long," Maria agreed. "I've been great! I saw your YouTube video with Tony and Luca, and I have to say, I'm so impressed and so proud of you."

Maria has always been supportive of me, and she is always encouraging me to be the best version of myself. She always offers to pick me up and drop me off whenever Mary and I hangout, and when we have sleepovers she never complains about how much noise we make. She treats me like family; embraces me as one of her own.

"Oh, thank you!" I was at a loss for words, and I wondered how many people in the Italian community had seen our video.

The four of us talked about how our dance class went before we eventually headed out the door. I said goodbye to Mary, and she wished me good luck with the boys tomorrow. In the car my mother talked about the events of her day. I listened to her and gave her advice on where to book in certain jobs and what number to quote the new ones that were booked in.

When I got home I immediately showered and went straight to bed. I smiled to myself as I thought about the girls at dance, and I wondered if any of them would sec the video. I was on my phone scrolling through social media, when I got a text from the group chat.

Tony: Do you guys want to come to my house tomorrow? Or are we going to Luca's?

Luca: Let's go to my house, I'm sure Lorenzo would want you guys over anway.

I chuckled to myself at the thought of Lorenzo clinging to my chest whenever he sat on my lap.

Me: *You guys should come over to my house. I feel bad that I've been to both of your houses, but you guys have not yet been over here.*

Tony: *No way I'm making my mom drive all the way down to the south part of the city.*

Me: *Worth a shot.*

Luca: *My house, 7:00pm. Don't be late this time, Gia.*

Me: *I'm never late!*

Tony: *You're always late.*

Luca: *Yeah, you're always late.*

Me: *Fine. I'll be there, see you then.*

Luca: *See you, guys.*

Tony: *Can't wait! It's going to be great!*

His enthusiasm made me laugh. Tony has always been the optimistic kind, but now he has turned into an energetic optimist. Although I love his energy, I wondered why he was so energetic at 11pm.

I tossed my phone gently on the ground and shut my eyes. I had a hard time falling asleep, so I started singing a traditional Italian lullaby, and soon enough, I was sleeping like a bear.

Chapter 14

"Look who showed up late," Luca jeered as I walked into his house. It was 7:02pm when I arrived at his house, so I just simply rolled my eyes and made my way over to Tony.

"Give it a rest," I pleaded as Tony hugged me tightly.

"Fine," Luca agreed as he hugged me as well. It was surprisingly quiet in his house, and I knew that we were the only ones home.

"When is Lorenzo going to be here?" I asked, wanting to give him his gift I had brought him.

"He'll be home in about thirty minutes, why?"

I walked over to my purse that I had laid down on their bench in the front room, and pulled out a wooden figure of a bear that stood on its two hind legs and read *Cutie Pie* on its belly. The bear caught my eye in our local market, and I thought I would get one for Lorenzo.

"Where'd you get it?" Tony asked, taking the bear into his palm and inspecting it closely.

"Just from Rexall, I got it on the way over here."

"Is that why you were late?"

I rolled my eyes. "I was only two minutes late!"

"He's going to love it," Luca assured me. "Let's go downstairs."

I followed the boys closely behind as their hair bounced up and down with every step they took. We plopped down on his sectional simultaneously and Tony was quickly pulling up our YouTube video.

"We're up to 760 views and 317 comments," he said, and I was shocked yet again. "I need to take this." Tony flipped his phone towards us and we saw his mother's name displayed on the screen before he left the room to talk to Susana.

"What's that about?" Luca asked, his words stern.

"What?" I had no idea what he was talking about.

"You tell me the other night that you don't want to get involved in a relationship with me, and now you're buying gifts for Lorenzo," he bellowed, his nostrils flaring out.

I stuttered, "I just wanted to do something nice for him." Looking back, it was probably a poor choice to buy Lorenzo a gift, but I wanted to make Enzo happy. I didn't even realise that Luca would take it this way. Now it just looked like I was playing with Luca's emotions, and I hated that.

"What's the matter with you?" He kept his voice low, but his words were still harsh. "Do you know how many times Lorenzo has come up to me and told me that I should ask you out?" Shit. I didn't know that. "Now he's going to constantly pester me about asking you out."

"Why are you so mad?"

"Because you just see me as a brother and Lorenzo sees you as his soon-to-be-sister-in-law, so what are you going to do?"

"I'm going to give him his gift." I stood my ground and I was not budging. "You can take this anyway you want it, but all I wanted to do was give a small gift to your younger brother because I love him."

"What gift?" Lorenzo and Tony asked, entering the room at the same time.

I reached into my purse and took out the bear. "This is for you."

"I love it, I love it, I love it!" Lorenzo gushed as he reached over to take the bear from me. "Thank you so much!" He hugged me closely before he examined the bear closely. Warm feelings swelled up inside me as I watched him inspect his new bear. He traced his fingers along the words *Cutie Pie* and smiled brightly as he met my eyes.

It brings me joy whenever I give people gifts. It was like saying thank you for all that they have done for me. I loved to hand people unexpected gifts and see the look on their faces. I always wanted people to know that I appreciate them, and it also gives me a reason to go shopping. Sometimes, I don't intend to buy anything for someone at all, but when something catches my eye and I am reminded of a certain person, I simply buy it. I hated mailing out gifts, though, I always loved to see their genuine reaction whenever they received my gift, and it makes me feel good when I make somebody's day just a little bit better.

"Lorenzo, go upstairs," Luca demanded and Enzo just gave him a cold look.

"Why?" He pouted, sinking deeper into my lap.

"Because Tony, Gia, and myself are going to start working on another video."

We are? What song?

"Fine," he said. "But just know this: I'm only leaving because I think that you guys will make it in the big leagues."

"Are we seriously going to do another cover?" Tony asked once Lorenzo, against his will, went upstairs.

"I was hoping we would." Luca glanced over at us with pleading eyes. Although I was a little pissed off at him right now, I couldn't resist those puppy dog eyes.

"What song should we sing this time?" I asked. I did not want to do another One Direction song because then people will start to think that we only listen to them.

"How about *Grenade* by Bruno Mars?" Tony proposed. I knew that song by heart, and I knew that we would all sound amazing when we sang it.

"Yes,T, great answer!" I clapped my hands and Tony laughed to himself while he shook his head.

"I like that song, too," Luca declared as grabbed Tony's phone to set it up. We practiced singing different parts of the song before we actually started to record it. I was surprised with how our voices blended together majestically and how well this song fit our voices. Finally, we were all satisfied with each other and decided to start filming. Tony placed his phone down on a ledge and hit the timer button and joined us quickly in the frame.

My heart was beating loudly and I wondered if the boys could hear it, but I was calmer than I was the first time we made a cover video. I wondered if the boys were more at ease with this as well, but before I could ask them Tony started singing.

Tony's voice sounded angelic as usual and I was, once again, in awe of him. Although I could only see the back of him, I could hear his smile with every word he sang.

Luca inhaled and started his verse, and Tony returned to stand next to me. Luca came in right on time and stayed perfectly in tune, and soon enough the chorus would start. I started to get nervous because the boy's solos sounded amazing, and I was worried I would ruin it.

We all sang as we breathed deeply from our diaphragms. The three of us sounded heavenly. I knew that we genuinely did make a good trio. The chorus started to come to an end; my solo was coming up soon.

The words escaped from my mouth smoothly as I stepped away from the boys. Once again, everything went black and I only focused on the lyrics and looking at the camera. My solo lasted about five or some lines before the boys joined in again. We harmonized with each other at the end, and soon enough Tony was running over to stop the video.

Thankfully, I did not collapse on the floor this time. Instead, I jumped into Luca, and he wrapped his arms around my back as I wrapped my

legs around his hips. He let out a chuckle as I
untangled myself from that position and blushed
profusely.

"Sorry," I said as I made my way over to
Tony. Tony quickly hugged me and then went
straight back to upload our video to YouTube.
"How many views does our first video
have?" Luca asked, refusing to make eye contact
with me.

"Oh. My. Gosh." Tony clapped his hands
together after every word he said. The anticipation
was internally killing me as I waited for Tony to stop
being dramatic and to expand on his idea. Finally,
he opened his mouth. "We have 1,500 views."

What?

Everything went blurry, I tried to look at
Luca, but he was only a spinning image. I looked
over at Tony, but I could not make out any of his
features. "Giovanna…" I was not sure who said my
name and I wasn't sure what else they said
because my head was pounding. It was good news,
why was I feeling awful right now? I stumbled
backwards, outstretching my arm to find a couch to
hold onto, except that there was no couch behind

me. I tried to speak, but my mouth was too dry. It just made a gasping noise.

"Guys?" I tried to say, but I was sure the boys could no longer make out what I was saying. Everything around me was spinning, so I closed my eyes. That was stupid of me. I lost consciousness; the only thing I felt was the warm carpet on my back.

Chapter 15

"Giovanna?" A voice wavered.

"Giovanna, wake up!" Another voice asked, their voice breaking in the process. I slowly started to open my eyes. The two voices let out a relieved sigh as a blob of brunette hair picked me up.

"What happened?" My voice was soft and delicate.

"You passed out. You were only out a couple of minutes, though."

"Tony?" I was still unsure of who answered my question.

"Yeah, it's me." His voice was sympathetic as he had me draped in his arms. "Luca! Get over here with the cloth!" His voice pierced through my mind.

"Tony," I scolded as he apologized softly while he brushed my curls away from my face and behind my ear.

"I'm here!" Luca announced as Tony gently placed me down on the couch while Luca rushed over and placed a cool cloth on my forehead. I smiled weakly at the boys who were leaning into me, only an inch away from my face.

"Sorry," I said as I looked up at their worried faces. "I didn't mean to scare you, it just happens from time to time." The boys did not back away, as they were still clearly worried about my well being.

"Are you going to be okay?" Luca asked, his voice shaking.

"I'll be fine."

"Do you want to go home?" Tony suggested.

I shook my head, but did not have the energy to speak anymore. The boys just nodded their heads understandingly and continued to dab the damp cloth around my forehead. Tony knelt down beside me and Luca copied his action. It felt a bit weird to see them on edge, I've never seen them like this before. After a couple of minutes, I finally found the energy to start speaking again. "Don't worry, I'm fine," I assured them, but they did not seem so convinced. "Like I said, it happens all the time. Besides, I probably just forgot to take a couple of my iron supplements. Anywho, so our video has over a thousand views!" I tried to lighten the mood, but the boys were still kneeling and squeezing my hand every now and then.

"Yea, 1,500 last time I checked before you-" Tony stopped his sentence and just looked at me sympathetically. I appreciated how the boys were genuinely worried about me, but I was fine.

"That's amazing!" I added with slightly more enthusiasm to show them that I was okay.

"Giovanna, you really scared us," Luca whispered, still not making eye contact with me.

"I'm sorry," I started, but Luca raised his hand up to shush me.

"No, no, you can't control when and where you pass out. We're not mad at you or anything, but we just got really freaked out." I could hear the worry in his voice.

"How often does this happen?" Tony questioned.

"To be honest, I'm not sure. I think it happens around once every two or three months. There is, really, nothing to worry about." I looked at them with an assuring look on my face. "I promise." That seemed to help the boys calm down a bit, because they know that I always keep my promises. I changed the subject onto our video and asked if Tony got our new video uploaded. Even though we changed subjects, the boys were eyeing me with caution.

"What time is it?" Tony asked.

"9:45pm." Luca responded, walking over to the fridge to bring me an ice cold water bottle.

"What time are your parents coming, Giovanna? Do you need my parents to drive you home?" Tony offered.

"They said they were coming at 10:00pm, so I don't think I need a ride." Tony seemed discouraged. "I'll let you know if I need one, though. Thanks for the offer." That seemed to brighten him up a bit, and I was glad.

"So, do you need us to carry you upstairs?" Luca asked, but never waited for my response as I was already being draped over the boys.

"I can walk," I assured them, and let go of each of their shoulders, but I ended up stumbling over myself.

"Oh for crying out loud, Giovanna, don't be stubborn."

"I'm not stubborn!" I defended, but I knew that it was true. I have always been set in my ways and I tended to refuse help when I needed it.

"Come here," Tony instructed. I was standing weakly between the two boys; my arms draped on each of their shoulders as if they were a pair of crutches. We headed for the stairwell, and took a significant amount of time in between each step. Eventually, the boys and I made it up the stairs and were greeted by worried looks from Giancarlo and Anna.

"What is going on? Are you hurt? Are you drunk? I told you, Luca, no drinking tonight!" Giancarlo questioned right away. The amount of questions he asked made my head hurt as I tried to explain, and I just ended up staring blankly at Luca and Tony.

"Giovanna passed out," Luca explained. "She keeps saying she's fine, but she could barely walk." Well, when he put it like that it made it seem like I was being dramatic, but I really was not. It grinded on me that I tried my best and I could not manage to gain my balance.

"Oh my gosh, I'm so sorry. Come, sit down." I obedy Giancarlo, and the boys guided me towards a long couch. As soon as I was seated, the faint sound of their doorbell went off. My shoulders deflated; it took so much energy and strength to get onto the couch and now I would have to get into my car.

"Stay here," Anna instructed as she made her way to the door. I glanced at Giancarlo who had a concerned look on his face, and I gave him a tired smile. He knew me all too well to know that I was not okay, and I loved and hated him for it.

"Giovanna?" My dad's voice was higher than usual.

"Hey, Pa," I said weakly, giving him the same tired smile.

"You passed out I heard, do you think you're going to be able to make it to the car?"

"Yeah, I'll be fine." I was about to get up when Tony locked his hand on my wrist and dragged me back to a seating position. "You. Can't. Walk. By. Yourself." His words were laced with concern. I glanced up at my dad who just nodded his head in agreement with Tony. I tried to silently ask Gian to defend me, but he was on his way to help me get up. This time, I was in between Giancarlo and my dad, and I heard them speaking in Italian.

"*Che è successo?*" My dad asked.

"*Non lo so,*" Giovanni responded, my dad gave him a look that said *Are you sure?*

"*È vero,*" I assured him. "He does not know what happened, and I don't even know what happened. Please, can you guys talk in English, it takes too much energy to switch between languages."

"Sorry, G," My dad said when we finally got down the front steps.

"No, it's okay," Giancarlo assured him.

"This happens all the time, and it's starting to worry us."

"Dad, I'm fine," I tried to bud in.

"Yeah, have you guys gone to a doctor?" Giancarlo asked, the both of them ignoring my efforts to convince them.

"We have, and they think it's just because she gets bad vertigo," My dad explained. "I guess she should blame me, I have always gotten bad vertigo, and like father like daughter." He winked at me, and for the first time since I passed out, I genuinely smiled. The two of them somehow managed to pick me up and placed me gently into the car seat. They quietly continued to chat between the two of them, but their words were muffled because they had closed the car door on me. Once my dad had gone in the car, I rolled down my window and weakly waved goodbye to Tony and Luca, who were still standing at the doorway. I felt a tad embarrassed that the boys had to see me so helpless and defenseless, but I knew they were understanding. My dad slowly drove off, and I tilted my head back on its rest.

"Are you okay?" My dad asked me, turning the radio down low.

"Yeah, I'm fine. I love you."

"I love you, bella." My dad glanced over at me, and I could feel my eyes start to shut. "It's okay, close your eyes and get some rest," My dad assured me. I listened to him, and I quickly fell into a deep sleep.

Chapter 16

I awoke to my dog barging into my room. I knew instantly that my dad must have picked me up and brought me to my bed because when I looked at my door it was creaked open, and he never closes the door fully. Remy jumped onto my bed and sniffed every inch of my face. I reached out to pet him, my arm feeling surprisingly stronger than it had felt yesterday, and rubbed him behind his ears. Remy snuggled closer to me as I pulled my blanket away from me.

I was still in my track pants and vibrant yellow T-Shirt that I wore to Luca's house the night before. I moved Groovy Bear to make more room for Remy as he continued to sniff my face and positioned himself so I could give him a belly rub. I reached over and picked up my phone where I saw various messages from the boys.

Tony: Let us know when you get home.

Luca: Yeah, and let us know how you are feeling.

I wondered if the boys were still worried about me because they sent those texts at night. I quickly sat up, shocking Remy in the process, and typed as fast as my little sausage fingers would allow me.

Me: I'm so sorry, I just woke up. I fell asleep as soon as my dad drove off, and I'm still in my clothes from yesterday. I'm fine, haven't tried walking though, but I have gained some of my strength back.

I sent the text and swung my legs over my bed, mentally preparing myself to get up and walk downstairs as if nothing happened. I glanced back at Remy who was still laying like a prince on my bed and smiled at him. *Here goes nothing.* I thought to myself as I placed one foot on the ground.

I badly wanted to just spring to my feet and devour breakfast, but I had to pace myself. I gently brought my other foot to the ground and slowly rose to my feet. I held onto my head board for balance and I was shocked at how stable I was. A proud smile made its way onto my face as I walked over to my dresser to get changed.

I got changed into a pair of black workout shorts and a grey tank top, and I decided to keep the boys updated.

Me: I just walked no problem! No need to worry.

I made my way downstairs where I was greeted right away by my mother. "How are you feeling?" She asked, embracing me in a tight hug.

"I'm doing so much better than yesterday. I can walk on my own now, so that's always a positive thing," I chuckled as I untangled myself from my mothers tight grip.

"Your father told me what happened, and you were completely knocked-out when he brought you to your bedroom, so I was really freaked out all night. I wanted to come check in on you, but I didn't want to bother you and I wanted you to rest."

"I'm sorry I made you worry, and if you checked in on me, it would be no bother to me."

"Oh no, there is no need for you to be sorry. I just wish there was something I could do to help you." I have done a lot of things to make my mother upset, like staying out later than I was supposed to, or not doing the laundry whenever she asked me to, but making her feel like she is helpless hit me the hardest.

I look up to my mother; she's my role model. I have seen her multitask like nobody else. The business phone would be ringing and she would be cooking and handling a customer simultaneously. I want to be like my mother when I grow up, I want to be strong just like her. I wish I could be more like her, and I wish I wouldn't give her such a hard time.

I've never been good at expressing my love for somebody, perhaps that is why I've never been in a relationship, so I end up picking on the people I love. I make fun of every little thing they do, right down to every hand movement they make. I wanted to tell my mother how much she meant to me, but I just could not. I was astonished with how hard it is for me to tell my family that I love them, but I could say those three little words to Tony and Luca without trouble.

"Breakfast?" I asked, finally breaking the silence. My mother led me to the table where she had laid out a fest for me. I saw fresh cut berries in a glass bowl and two slices of french toast.

"Antonio!" My mother screeched. I cringed at her loud, high pitched voice, but decided that I should not comment on it and continue to eat.

"What?" My brother yelled from another room.

"Come here!" My mother demanded in her nasally voice. I could hear my brother's footsteps quicken as he approached our table.

"Giovanna!" My brother exclaimed as soon as he caught sight of me. He came over to my chair and we did our original handshake. "What's up with my *sorella*?"

"Nothing, my *fratello*."

"What did you need, mamma?"

"Can you go upstairs and get me my hair elastic?" My mother asked. My brother and I shared a confused, annoyed glance at each other.

"You brought me into another room, made me stop my show, just to get you a hair elastic?" My brother asked, clearly bothered as he tried to make sense of my mother's logic.

"Yes," My mother said as she tossed her head to the side and smiled brightly. Sometimes I wonder what goes on in her head, some of the things she says make no sense. However, my brother did not argue further and dashed up the stairs. He returned within seconds and handed my mother a black elastic. My mother quickly tied up her tight curls into a small bun on the crown of her head and continued to wash the dishes.

"Mom, I have a question," I asked suddenly once my brother returned to wherever he was before.

"Yeah, what?"

"Do you think this is stupid?" I asked weakly.

"What's stupid?" She did not look up at me, even though I was staring directly at her. She was busing herself with making the pans sparkly clean.

"This whole thing I'm doing with Tony and Luca."

My mother still did not meet my gaze as she responded, "No." I was expecting her to give an explanation, but she just went back to silently doing the dishes.

"No?" My voice came out shakier than I intended it to.

"No, I don't think it's stupid. In fact, I think you guys will genuinely make it in the industry." Her kind words shocked me, and I was speechless. I always knew my mother was supportive after she saw our video, but I did not expect her to be this supportive of Insieme. I was expecting her to tell me to focus on my schoolwork, or to not get my hopes up. My mother finally met my eyes and saw my shocked expression. "Don't look at me like that," she laughed.

"You really think we'll be alright?"

"Giovanna, let me tell you something." She turned off the running water and dried her hands quickly before she sat in a chair across from me. "I always knew you wanted more than this." She raised her hands into the air to get her point across. "I know that you're uncertain of what job career you should take, and don't get me wrong you are still getting educated, but I knew that you craved, longed, for something more than an ordinary job. Giovanna, I want you to know that I support you no matter what. Even if this whole situation does not work out in your favor, I'm proud of you." I was taken aback by her words. That's all I ever wanted: to make my mother proud. My shoulders relaxed as my mother continued to speak to me. "Do you know that? Do you know that I'm proud of you, I mean."

"Yes," I managed to muster up, but could not say anything more.

"You don't know how much respect I have for you; I would never put myself out there like that. Whenever I go grocery shopping, or I'm at your dance studio, people are always telling me how impressed they were with your video. I feel like the whole Italian community has seen it."

"That's a good thing," I laughed. My mother and I continued to talk about how well our video was doing, and I informed her that we uploaded a new video. I also told her that I was planning on seeing the boys again soon. She was over the moon once she watched our second video, and eventually she had to leave to answer the ringing business phone.

My phone buzzed quietly and I had received another text from Tony.

Tony: That's amazing! I'm so glad to hear that!

I smiled at Tony's message, knowing that he was genuinely happy for me.

Luca: Me too, I was so worried about you. Take a look at this, Giovanna. He attached a photo to our group chat. Tony and Luca were sitting in the back seat of a car with bright smiles on their faces.

Tony's deep hazelnut eyes were sparkling vibrantly as the sunshine hit his face just right. He was grinning, showing off his straight teeth, and he was in a plain T-shirt that matched his eye colour. Luca, who was closer to the front of the selfie, was wearing a baby pink shirt with tiny white birds spread all over his chest. He, too, was smiling a smile that could brighten a dark lit room. They looked joyful, and I could feel their positivity radiating from the picture.

Luca: *We're on our way to pick you up. Get ready, we'll be there in twenty minutes.*

Me: *Okay, sounds good.*

It was good, I was happy that I could see them again. I was curious as to what we would be doing, but I did not care, as long as I could see them I was happy.

"Mom," I called as soon as she was off the phone. "The boys are on their way to pick me up." My mother nodded and said that she was okay with me going out again. I quickly walked upstairs and got dressed, excited about what the boys had planned.

"Giovannaaa!" Tony sang as I ran out the front door and walked to their car. Susana was smiling as I jumped into her car.

"You guys!" I smiled back, laughing as I buckled my seatbelt. "How are we doing?"

"Oh, Gia! The sun is shining, we're going to get ice cream, we're on spring break, we're feeling fabulous!" Luca responded, winking at me.

"Luca, stop winking at me!"

"No, nice outfit, by the way."

"Thanks!" I responded. I was wearing loose fitting olive joggers and a short-sleeve white T-shirt with buttons going down the middle of my shirt.

"How are you doing?" Susana asked, looking at me with sympathy through her rearview mirror.

"I'm alright, I'm alright, I can't complain," I shrugged, which was true.

"So you pass out a lot?" She pressed as she switched lanes.

"Mom!" Tony condemned as he rolled his eyes.

"No, it's okay, Tony," I assured him with a slight nod. "Yeah, sometimes my vertigo gets really bad and I just end up passing out. I can't control when it happens, but I seem to be getting better." I tried to sound chipper as I adjusted my loose bun.

"What is your favourite ice cream flavour?" Tony asked, changing the subject while he shot his mother an annoyed look.

"Cookie-dough!" Luca exclaimed. "It's so good, it's a bit basic, but I like the classics. I will not tolerate people sending hate to cookie-dough ice cream."

"Mint-chocolate chip," I stated. The boys gave me a disgusted and confused look. "What?"

"You," Tony rested his hand on his chin while he found the right words. "Do you actually like mint-chocolate chip?"

I nodded my head. I was not quite sure what was so hard to understand, I loved it and that was that.

"Are you kidding me?" Luca asked, "It's like eating toothpaste!" Tony nodded in agreement as they continued to share a concerned look.

"What! No it does not!" I defend. I caught sight of Susana in the mirror, her lips were pursed together as if she was trying to hold in her laugh. I could see her eyes raise up as she held in her laughter and shook her head.

"What's so funny, Susana?" I laughed.

"It's just," she finally let her lips lose and let out a contagious laugh. "You guys sound like five year olds."

"I just simply don't understand how Giovanna can like such a disgusting thing," Tony stated.

"I like you, don't I?" I fired back. The whole car erupted with roaring laughter. Luca was doubled-over and Susana was shaking uncontrollably. I even saw Tony let out a few chuckles. We continued our silly debate amongst ourselves before Susana pulled up to the ice cream parlor. She dropped us off and explained that she would be back to pick us up in about three hours and we should walk around the area a bit.

"You guys go get a picnic table, I'll go get the ice cream cups," Tony instructed.

"Sounds good, here you go." I placed enough money to cover my ice cream in his palm, but he refused it and insisted that he would pay for all of us. I finally agreed and Tony went inside the shop while Luca and I tried to find a table.

"How have you been, and don't say you're okay, how have you actually been?" Luca questioned as we finally found an open picnic table.

"I've been good," I stated, but only got a raised eyebrow from Luca in return. "I mean it," I defend.

"You don't have to act tough when you're around me. You can say whatever is on your mind, I just want to make sure you are alright." I was taken aback by his kind words, and I decided that maybe I should open up to him more.

"Well, I guess, I'm just tired," I stated, nodding his head as he asked me to continue. "I feel like I have so much pressure put on me, not by anybody, but I feel like I'm putting so much pressure on myself. It's hard to explain," I said, dropping my shoulders in defeat.

"No, I understand." Luca reached out and squeezed my hand gently. Usually, I would snatch my hand away, but I didn't this time.

"This whole Insieme thing, I keep wondering if it will work out. My family, your family, Tony's family, all believe in us, but I don't even know if I believe in myself. Sometimes I wish that I would be like my brother, already know what I'm going to do with my life and have an actual plan. I guess I just don't want to get anybody's hopes up, especially mine." I hung my head.

"I don't know what the future holds for the three of us," Luca admitted. "I know that we will always have each other, though. Maybe we won't be selling out stadiums, or realising original albums, but we'll have each other. If you had not approached me about joining the trio, I probably would have still been training for football."

"You're not training for football anymore?" I interrupted, shocked at what he just said.

"I mean, I am." He dropped his head. "Just not as heavily. Before the whole Insieme situation, I was certain that the only way I would get into post-secondary education was to receive a scholarship. I put loads and loads of pressure on me, just like you're doing now, and I trained everyday. I never had a rest day, I just wanted to be better."

"Luca," I started sympathetically, but he just carried on.

"You, and only you, have taught me that I am more than just a game. I'm more than just a dumb football player. For a long time I believed that I was genuinely just meant to play football. Don't get me wrong, I don't think football players are dumb, but I felt like I was dumb. If you had not come into my life, I would still be miserable. I would still be self-conscious of my every move. For you, I'm forever grateful." He was staring into my soul with his big brown eyes, and for a moment I wanted to reach over and embrace him. I wanted to let him know that everything will be okay. I wanted to let him know that he has taught me so much. I wanted to tell him how I felt like he was my brother, but I did not know where to start. We sat there in silence for a short period of time before the two of us heard a faint voice.

"Hello?" A girl who looked like she was only eleven or twelve years of age walked up towards our table. I instantly let go of Luca's hand and turned my attention towards her; Luca copied my actions.

"I'm sorry," she said as she walked closer to us. "I have a question for you both." She glanced between the two of us, and my heart was pounding so loud that I was certain she could hear.

"Yeah, anything," Luca responded calmly.

"Are you guys Insieme?"

Chapter 17

"I'm back!" Tony announced as he approached our table, but stopped dead in his tracks as he realized we were staring dumbfounded at a stranger. He joined us, placing three cups of ice cream down.

"You're part of Insieme, too!" The young girl noticed. Tony's mouth dropped to the ground, just like Luca and I did.

"You," Luca started, but stopped, unsure of what to say. What were we supposed to say? Had our video really taken off that strangers in the city could recognize us? I glanced over at my ice cream, longing for it to comfort my nerves.

"How did you," Tony tried to ask her, but was at a loss for words.

"I saw you guys on YouTube," The girl answered the question that was hanging in the air like an elephant in a room. The three of us looked at each other silently, waiting for somebody to say anything.

"I'm a big fan."

What?! A million fireworks went off inside me as joy swept over me overwhelmingly. I wanted to jump up and hug her, and I did just that. Before I could think, I sprang to my feet and embraced the young girl in a tight hug.

"You don't know how much that means to me!" I explained, pulling back and keeping her at arm's length.

"I saw your video, and I have to say, I fell in love instantly," she laughed and beamed at me. "The way you guys harmonize heavenly and effortlessly and you guys just seem so, so natural."

Luca and Tony were still sitting, so she walked over and gave them a hug. The boys were still in shock, but they wrapped their arms around the little girl.

"Please, realise more covers. Realise your own songs!" She encouraged us.

"What is your name?"

"Diana," she said proudly, extending an arm out for the three of us to shake. I took her hand gently. "Can I take a photo of the four of us?"

"What?" Luca asked, and Tony punched him lightly on the shoulder.

"You want a photo with us?" I asked, not comprehending what she was asking. Diana simply nodded her hand and pulled out her phone from her back pocket. She extended the arm that held her phone out in front of her, while Tony, Luca, and myself crammed into the picture frame. With her free hand, Diana pointed behind her to the three of us. She smiled brightly as if she just met Santa Clause, and her radiant smile took up the whole picture. I smiled widely, trying to keep from freaking out at the fact that a stranger knew who I was, who we were.

Once she snapped a photo she turned around to see our surprised expressions.

"What? Was that the first photo you've ever taken with a fan?"

"We don't really have fans, so yeah, you were the first person," I admitted, still finding it hard to believe that she considered herself a fan.

"What do you mean 'We don't really have fans'?" She mocked me as she shook her head. "Have you not seen your YouTube video? You guys are now around four thousand views, and I don't even think I've seen one hate comment." I flinched a little because I knew her statement was false. Sonia had left a hate comment, and I would soon have to face her at school and I was dreading it. However, I was also ecstatic to know that we were now around four thousand views.

"We have how many views now?" Tony asked, giving Luca and I a shocked look.

"Four thousand. Are you hard of hearing, Tony?"

"You know my name?"

She knows Tony's name?

"Of course, I know all of your names. Tony, Luca, and Giovanna!" She stated, pointing to each of us as she recalled our names. "Well, I have to get going now, but it was lovely meeting you guys. I love you guys! Don't forget me when you're selling out stadiums!" And before we could tell her how much we appreciated her words, she took off. The three of us stood there trying to process what had just happened.

"Wow," Luca finally said, making his way back over to the table, Tony and I following closely behind.

"I was not expecting that," I admitted, but then again, what was I expecting? I knew that this is what I wanted, I wanted to be known in the world, so why is it so hard for me to comprehend that Diana is a fan?

"Me too," Tony said. It was hard for me to believe that a stranger knew our names, and she liked our singing voices. It was one thing if our family and friends saw our video and commented on how well we sounded together, but it was another thing if someone who we have never met before called themselves a fan of our work. We don't even have any original songs out, and we only have two videos on our channel.

"Did you guys catch that we have around four thousand views now?" Luca wondered out loud, clearly proud of our accomplishments.

"Hard to believe," Tony and I said at the same time.

"Do you really think we should make our own songs?" Luca asked. That was a great question, and I did not yet know the answer. I would write a few songs here and there, but nothing extraordinary. Sometimes writing simple song lyrics was the only way I knew how to cope with my pain, and I have some good ideas about what to write about.

"I think we should take things slow, maybe release more covers and then see where that takes us," Tony suggested. "Besides, I don't know how to write a song."

"I can write a song," I blurted. I slapped my hand to my mouth, unsure of why I just put myself out there like that.

"You can?" They both asked.

"I mean, not good ones, but I have some good ideas," I admitted, mentally kicking myself for putting even more pressure on me.

"Well, my mom is going to be here soon so let's finish our ice cream. How about we all go home and try and write a few songs of our own, and then we can share them with each other." I nodded slowly, even though I had no clue where to start for an original song.

I pushed the uneasy emotions down as the boys and I ate our ice cream. We discussed how crazy it was that we had a fan and how excited we were to continue to upload more videos. Luca and Tony were still giving me a hard time about ordering mint ice cream, but I just told them that they were missing out.

It was a beautiful day, the sun was shining
and the birds were chirping, but that still did not
stop the churning in my stomach. I had a mix of
excitement, nervousness, and doubt inside me. I
was excited that someone recognized us, but I was
nervous that people would not like us. Maybe Sofia
would not be the only one to leave a hate comment
on our postings. I wanted to put myself out there,
but doubt started to kick in. Maybe I'm not cut out
for this, whatever this is. I should be focusing on
raising my school grades, not putting all my energy
into Insieme.

I love the boys, and it was clear that they
care deeply about me, but I was not sure that I
wanted this. Perhaps the boys were feeling some
sort of doubt themselves, but it was my idea and if
we fail I will never be able to forgive myself. It was
me who had the dream, me who brought the idea to
them, but it was them who started to turn that single
dream into reality.

I started to reminisce about the Drive-In,
and I wondered if I would be here today if I had not
bumped into Tony. The truth is, I probably would not
have even talked to the boys if I did not see Tony

that day. I would have kept my dream a secret, and that secret would eat me up late at night. I was thankful that I saw Tony, but I was more thankful that he did not laugh in my face. Sometimes whenever I tell an individual about my certain hopes and dreams, they just brush it off. I vividly remember the hopeful look in Tony's eyes that day, I remember how he jumped into this without looking back. I longed to be like that, to have zero worries about failing. That day, Tony had been so sure that this would work out, and it was so encouraging to see that. The fact of the matter is: if it were not for Tony, then I would still be locked in my room daydreaming about being known.

I finished my ice cream and glanced up at Tony with a slight smile on my face. I wanted to tell him how much he has done for me because I'm not sure he realizes how much he has impacted my life. He has changed my life forever.

"Are you alright?" Tony asked, snapping me out of my thoughts.

"Yeah, I'm just tired," I said. I really wanted to let him know what I was thinking about, but I could not. Maybe it was because of my lack of communication skills; I just couldn't put into words how much he meant to me.

"Me too," Tony agreed. "Look, my mom is here! Let's go."

The three of us squeezed our way into Susana's car where we fought over who got to select the music. Unfortunately, Luca ended up taking the aux cord and we had to sit through heavy rap. I don't mind rap, but Luca put on very heavy, hardcore, rap music. It was giving me a headache, but thankfully Susana turned it down a bit.

"How was your ice cream?" She asked.

"We met a fan," Tony blurted out, staring directly out his window. It still shocked me that Diana considered herself a fan.

"What?" Susana snapped her head around, nearly shifting into a different lane as she did so.

"Mom, watch the road!" Tony instructed as he laughed.

"You're right, I'm sorry," she said, focusing her eyes back onto the road ahead of her. "Sorry, you said that you met a fan? What do you mean by that?" Tony, Luca, and I explained what happened in our encounter with Diana. We explained how she wanted a picture and how she recognized us from a mile away. Susana was over the moon, perhaps more excited than the three of us. We eventually arrived at my house first and I thanked her for driving me.

"Giovanna," Tony said, stopping me as I opened the car door. I turned around, waiting for him to continue. "Thank you," He finally said.

"For what?" I asked, shifting back into my seat so I could look right into his eyes.

"This would not be possible if it weren't for you." I could see Luca nodding his head as well.

I smiled brightly before I got out of the car before I turned around and said, "That's where you're wrong, Tony." I could see the confused expression on his face, but I just gently shut the door and smiled in his face. As I walked away, Susana honked as she waved goodbye to me, and the boys waved as well. I entered my house where I was greeted by no one except my dog. Everyone must have been out, so I headed straight to my room and got out a pen and paper.

Tony,

When you told me that all of this is possible because of me, I couldn't believe it. I need you to know that this is all possible because of you. If you didn't bump into me at Lane's all those weeks ago, we wouldn't even be talking to each other right now. You are the reason that Insieme has four thousand views. Yes, I was the one who had the dream, but you're the one that made it turn into a reality. I am forever grateful for you, and I need you to know that I am always here for you. Please, listen to me when I tell you that I love you no matter what.

Love you forever,

Giovanna

I folded up the short and sweet note into a tiny envelope and wrote down his address. I changed into running attire and grabbed my headphones. I quickly said goodbye to Remy and ran out the door with the envelope in hand.

I started jogging down the street, gripping the envelope tightly, and made my way to the mailbox. My foot hit the pavement perfectly on time with the beat of whatever song came on shuffle, and my breathing was deep and steady. I finally made it to the mailbox and quickly slipped in my letter. After I was sure that the letter was completely in the box, I took off around my neighborhood.

Exercising was one of my favorite things to do. It helped me take my mind off of situations, and it was good for my mental health. Before I started working out, I was in a really bad mental health state. I was depressed, and I had no way of coping with my sadness. I felt like I had no friends, and, in a way, it was true.

Junior high school really impacted my life in a negative way. My classmates would constantly make fun of me and would find a way to point out my insecurities every chance they had. I would get made fun of for my size, and I remember people would tell me that I'm fat. For so long I believed them, and I always viewed myself as ugly. They would point out my acne, eye bags, and even the size of my knees. I tried to shrug off their comments, and I would remind myself that they have nothing better to do with their lives, but it was hard. It was hard to go through an eight hour school day where people would constantly mock and criticize me, and then come home and pretend that I thought I was pretty.

That led to me gaining bad habits. I let myself go, I would eat until I felt like throwing up, and I would not sleep, and I would yell and scream at my parents. I was never mad at my parents, but that was how I dealt with my stress. I knew my parents wanted what was best for me, and I hated myself for taking all my anger out on them.

However, in my grade nine year I decided that I could not maintain those bad habits. I started going to the gym, where I met my trainer who changed my life for the better. He reminded me that life was better when you smiled, and he reminded me that life is beautiful. He was one of those people that radiated positive energy, and I wanted to be exactly like him. He single handedly changed my life, and now here I am going on a run around my neighborhood.

I could feel the sadness start to well up inside me as I thought back to my junior high days, but I just focused on the pavement in front of me..

"Hello?" I heard somebody scream. I clicked on my headphones to pause my blaring music and looked up. I was right outside my high school, and on the school's lawn I saw the person who was waving me over. I was sceptical because our whole school was on spring break, and the figure seemed to be too short to be a teacher. The right thing to do was to turn around and sprint home, but I was never one to be logical, so I crossed the street towards the dark figure.

"Giovanna!" I heard an all too familiar voice call out. He was approaching me so I could make out his face, making my heart leap.

"Danny? What are you doing here?" I asked, raising my arms up at the school.

"I was playing at the tennis court with one of my friends, but he left and now I'm waiting for my mom," he explained. "What are you doing here?"

"I live in the area," I peeped.

"Come here," he said, extending his hand out, and without hesitation, I took his hand in mine.

I was curious as to where he was taking me, but I did not say anything. I could feel my cheeks flush, and I knew it was not because I had been running, it was because I was finally seeing Danny outside of class.

I never even knew who Danny was before science class. We sit next to each other, and that is the only reason why I bother to show up to science class. I did not see him the first day, but once we got our seating plan I noticed how cute he is.

Danny looks like me, maybe that's why I find him very cute. He has deep brown eyes that widen everytime he talks about something that interests him, and tanned olive skin that matches his dark brown curly hair. The thing I like about him the most, though, is that when his friends around him are being loud and obnoxious, he remains silent and sweet. I could feel my heart start to speed up with excitement as he led me to a bench around the corner.

"How are you?" He asked, as he pushed his brown curls away from his eyes.

"I'm doing pretty good, how are you?" I smiled.

"I'm pretty good as well, do you go on runs often?" He asked, looking at my outfit, and I could feel my cheeks burn like fire. I wish he would have stopped me when I was wearing a cute sundress, not when I was in running shorts and a workout top with my bun falling messily behind my head.

"Yeah, it takes my mind off of things for a while."

"Things," he said, staring deep into my eyes and making my heart do a backflip. "As in Insieme?"

"What?" I blurted, as I buried my face into the palms of my hands in embarrassment. "You know about that?"

"Of course, I even liked your guy's videos," he said proudly.

"Thank you."

"That's a pretty sick name, Insieme, I mean."

"Yeah, and I'm shocked that you're saying it right," I noted as I looked up at him again. This was the first time we were talking about something non-sports related, and that meant that I was automatically awkward and saying unnecessary things.

"Thank goodness," he laughed and so did I, but then there was a long period of silence. I got instantly nervous, unsure of what to say.

"Those boys," he started, but then shut his mouth and tried to find the right way to put this. "Those boys you were singing with in the video, are they? Nevermind." He shook his head.

"Are they what?" I pushed, scooching closer to him with compassion, shocking myself as I did so because usually I get all choked up around him.

"Are they, I don't know how to say this, do you like them?" He no longer met my eyes, despite my efforts to move closer to him.

"What do you mean?"

"Like, would you consider dating them?" He whispered, and I was shocked at how embarrassed he looked. His cheeks were flushed and he shook his foot viciously. He never looked embarrassed- he was always the calm, cool, collected guy- and now he was wondering if either Tony or Luca was my boyfriend or love interest. While Luca and I shared a kiss, Danny was my first priory and I would kiss Danny if I were sober, unlike Luca.

"No, not at all," I assured him, trying not to make it sound too obvious that I really like him. I thought I saw his face light up, but I shook the idea out of my head, knowing that he would never like me.

"Oh."

What does "Oh" mean? I wondered, but my thoughts stopped now that Danny was looking at me again.

"I need to tell you something," he finally announced, and I could feel my stomach drop. I nodded my head because I suddenly seemed to have magically lost my voice. "I know that we don't really know each other on a deeper level, but I feel like you understand me. Does that make sense? Like, whenever we talk about sports, it's like you already know what I'm going to say."

"Yeah, I feel the same way too," I said as he leaned in closer to me, putting his arm around the bench as I moved a little closer. Adrenaline surged through my veins, and I was silently praying that my deodorant would mask my body odor at the moment.

"Good, and I feel comfortable around you. Sometimes when my friends are being ignorant, I look over to you and I see you have a worried look on your face, and I'm glad to know that I'm not the only one who has a problem with how they talk to one another," he laughed, and I did the same thing, knowing that his friends truly did have some questionable moments. "The truth is, Giovanna, I really like you."

My heart stopped, and my mind went blank. Did Danny Garcia really like me? Was I hearing this right?

"When I saw your YouTube videos, I was impressed by how well you can sing, but I was devastated because I thought you were dating one of them," he carried on. "Giovanna, I know you probably do not feel the same way, but-"

"Danny," I leaned into him as I silenced him, and he wrapped his arms around me. "I like you, too."

"Really?" He asked shocked, and I was glad that I was not the only shocked one here.

"Of course," I smiled at him. "You really thought my singing was-"

Before I had a chance to ask him if he really liked Insieme, I was cut off by Danny's sudden movement. He had embraced me in his muscular arms and pressed his lips on mine. I did not know what was happening, but I think I kissed him back. I'm not sure, everything was a blur, and I was really nervous. He eventually pulled back and looked slightly down at me because of our height differences, and I could see a genuine smile spread across his face. He leaned next to my ear and whispered softly, "I'll text you." And he gave me a quick peck on my cheek before he hopped into his mother's car.

Chapter 18

"You're lying!" Mary screamed at me. Of course, I had to FaceTime my best friend and explain to her what just happened.

"Would I lie?" I laughed, burying my head into my hands as I thought about Danny. It all happened so fast, and I just couldn't believe that he liked me back. All those days of planning out my outfits, styling my hair differently, and talking endlessly about whatever sports game was on the day before, finally paid off. Danny Garcia liked me back.

"So are you guys dating now?" Mary asked, bringing her face as close to the screen as she possibly could.

"I don't know, but he texted me a few minutes ago," I shrugged.

"Have you responded?"

"No."

"What!?" She dropped her mouth to the ground. "Giovanna Rossi, if you don't respond to him this instant, I promise you that I will come over to your house and do it for you."

"Calm yourself, I'll respond right now," I said.

Danny: Hey Giovanna, I was just wondering if you would like to hangout sometime?

Me: Yes I would, what time were you thinking?

"What did he say?" Mary questioned immediately after hearing me send the text.

"Relax, Mary, I literally just sent him the text."

"Fine," she rolled her eyes, but then gasped instantly as she heard my phone ping to sound, giving away that Danny texted me back.

Danny: Are you free tomorrow?

"Mary, he's asking if I'm free tomorrow."

"Say you are! Don't fail on me now, Rossi."

Me: Yeah :)

Danny: Okay great, I'll pick you up around 4 and then we can go to the movies and walk around the mall.

Me: Sounds good, see you then!

"Okay, so he's picking me up tomorrow," I explained to my speechless best friend. "I have no idea what to wear."

"Wear that light blue dress that you just got," she said instantly. "The one with the white flowers on it. You look so good in that dress."

"Do you think it's too formal?"

"No, not at all," she expressed. "Oh shit, sorry Giovanna, I have to go now because my mom needs me. Tell me how it goes tomorrow, I love you."

"I love you."

As soon as Mary hung up I opened up my window and climbed onto the roof. I sat down, putting my earbuds in and looking up at the stars. I loved stargazing because it takes my mind off of all my worries, and I like to be alone sometimes. I was thinking about all that was going on right now. I checked Insieme's video and we were now at seven thousand views on our first video and about three thousand views on our latest one. I was ecstatic, and I wondered if things were going to pick up even more, and perhaps we could get a gig at my uncle's restaurant.

My thoughts were interrupted by a call from Jana.

"I saw your text, what's up?" She sounded tired, but yet she sounded interested.

"You know Danny?" I asked, barely holding in my enthusiasm.

"Danny," she pondered, and there was a long pause before I heard her gasp in realization. "Of course! Danny, the boy who you are so nervous to talk to but can't stop telling me about him. That Danny?"

I chuckled, "Yes, that Danny. Well, I was going on a run because I had to drop off a letter in the mail, and I bumped into him."

"He was in your neighbourhood?" She asked specticaly.

"Yeah, you know how I walk to school?"

"You remind me every day." I could hear her rolling her eyes through the phone.

"And you know how there are those tennis courts right next to our school?"

"Yes, you always tell me that we have to play tennis and then we never do."

"Yeah, those ones, he was playing tennis there and called me over."

"What?" She screamed, and I heard her slap her hand over her mouth. "What did he say?" She pressed.

"Long story short, we're going on a date to the movies tomorrow."

She was speechless, and I started laughing in hopes it would break the silence.

"What happened exactly, I need details!" She demanded. I rolled my eyes, but I told her every little detail there was to know.

"He kissed you!?" She exclaimed, and I had to pull my phone away from my ear because she screamed loudly with excitement.

The two of us continued to talk about Danny as I stared out to my empty neighbourhood, and she gave me advice on how to act. She has been in a relationship for about a year now, so she gave me key tips about what to say, when to laugh, when to brush his arm. The whole thing seemed silly, I wondered why I could not just be myself, but I listened to Jana carefully.

"So, I saw your video," she simply stated once she was done instructing me on how to act tomorrow.

"Really?" I asked, and I was surprised. I need to start getting used to the fact that people that I know have seen my YouTube video, but,still, it shocks me everytime.

"Yeah, I really liked it, Gia." It was a simple complement, but it made every bone in my body vibrate with joy. Maybe it was because Jana and I picked on each other every chance we got, and now she was supporting me. I've told her that I want more than this, and she's always been supportive, but now that she's actually seen the video she's even more excited.

Jana and I talked for hours as I looked up at the sky, and I even told her that I need to write an original song. Out of all the things that were going on in my life, that task scared me the most.

Jana told me that I need a good night's sleep so I can be on my best behaviour for tomorrow, and she ended the call. I silently slipped back into my room and cuddled tightly next to my teddy bear, dozing off instantly.

I awoke at dawn, rays of orange sunlight were beaming through my window, my stomach churning with nervousness, and headed downstairs. I was greeted by my whole family and they told me about their shopping experiences they had yesterday. I told them that Danny asked me out, leaving out the part where we shared a kiss, and my mother was so happy for me. Antonio, of course, encouraged me and asked what took so long.

My brother and I have always told each other everything going on in our lives. He knew that I've liked Danny for a while now, and he was the person I was most excited to tell. He had a hard time hiding his excitement, but he controlled himself around our father.

My dad, on the other hand, was not so ecstatic. I was nervous that he would say no like he did a year ago, but he just simply sat there. I waited for his approval, but he just stared at me blankly.

"Just be safe," he said, and I was not sure how to respond to that. However, we carried on and told each other stories about the night before.

It was finally time for me to get ready, as Danny would be arriving at my door around two o'clock, so I went to shower. I quickly hopped in the shower, rinsing my hair thoroughly with my oat scented shampoo. It was the fastest shower I've ever taken, but I was in a rush to get into my outfit.

After I quickly dried myself and put on my robe, I sprinted into my bedroom, immediately shutting the door behind me. I quickly jumped into the dress Mary and I had decided on, and rushed back into my bathroom. I gently unraveled the towel that I had wrapped around my damp hair and let it fall freely. I carefully brushed out my wet hair and then ran my product-covered fingers through my hair. I wrapped the towel around my hair again so I could do my makeup.

I was never one to wear loads of makeup, in fact, I would barely wear any makeup at all. Today, however, is a special occasion. I softly stroked my mascara brush onto my eyelashes, making them darker and longer than they already were. I gently applied a clear lip gloss over my freshly moisturized lips, and I also put on a hint of blush.

Once I let my hair free, I charged back into my room. I flung open my closet doors and started searching for my grandmother's pearl necklace and matching earrings. I finally found them and gently locked in the necklace around my neck, and clasped on the simple earrings.

My grandmother had given me a thin silver chain with a single pearl dangling at the bottom of it, with matching single pearled earrings. I wore the necklace and earrings for special occasions, and they somehow managed to calm me. It was like a piece of my grandmother was with me, and it was one of the only materialistic things I have left of her.

I stared at my reflection, and I felt gorgeous. This was the first time that I actually loved myself. My dress flowed naturally above my knee and hugged all of my body's curves just right. My curls were completely dry and hung just below my shoulder blades. I checked my freshly brushed teeth one last time to make sure nothing was stuck in between any small gaps. I was happy with my appearance, so I made my way downstairs.

I was talking with my brother, when all of a sudden I heard our doorbell ring. I sprang to my feet and rushed over to open the door.

"Hi, Giovanna," Danny said happily as soon as I walked through the door, not bothering to wave goodbye to my parents or Antonio.

"Hey," I trembled, immediately clearing my throat in hopes it would change my voice back to normal. I started to remember the advice Jana had given me: act like you know what you're doing.

"How was your night?" He asked, opening the car door for me.

"It was pretty nice, I didn't really do anything," I shrugged as I said hello to his mother. His mother was very pretty, and Danny was a spitting image of her, but she was very intimidating. I smiled at her, but she returned my smile with a stern look. I shot Danny a nervous glance, and he just simply shrugged as if it was normal.

The car ride there was awkward, and I knew instantly that his mother did not like me. The tension in Danny's SUV was so tight you could cut it with a knife. I truly did want to be anywhere but in that car, and I was hoping that things would get better as the night went on.

"You were quiet in the car, is everything alright?" Danny asked after he got us our tickets. I have to admit, I was pleasantly surprised with how much of a gentleman he is. He's done everything right today, from opening the car door for me, to paying for the movie tickets and concession. Me, on the other hand, I've only managed to make his mother hate me and make my voice sound shaky.

"Yeah, sorry," I shrugged, and I could hear Jana's advice play over and over again in the back of my mind like a broken record. I wanted to follow her advice, but I was too nervous to.

"My mother is nice, trust me, it just takes some time for her to open up to new people," he explained, as if he could clearly read my mind. I did not want to bash his mother, so I just simply smiled and moved onto another topic.

"Thank you for paying," I said, and he just brushed it off like it was nothing. "No, seriously, it means alot to me." I reached over and gave his shoulder a small squeeze- following Jana's advice- which seemed to have made him happy.

We made our way to our seats, which were the very last row in the theater. The rest of the theater was packed with people, but we had our row all to ourselves. The movie started to play, but I did not really pay much attention to what was happening on the big screen. The truth is, I don't even know the name of the movie we were watching. I kept looking over Danny, and sometimes we would make eye contact and I would look away in embarrassment. His arm was draped around me and I was close to him, the only thing separating us from me snuggling up onto his chest was the armrest. However, he squeezed my shoulder gently, but tightly, and I inched closer towards him. When I looked up at him again, I saw his pearly white teeth smiling down at me, and I returned his smile with a wide grin of my own. I wanted the movie to be over soon so I could spend the rest of the evening talking with him.

My mind was swarming with thoughts about Danny, and, of course, Jana's wise words. I was debating what to talk about once the movie was finished. I thought I had more time to figure out some sort of topic to discuss, but when I focused back on the screen, the ending credits were displayed. I could feel my heart start to speed up as Danny locked his hand in mine and we walked out.

"Did you like the movie?" He asked once we started walking around the mall.

"Yeah, it was pretty good," I lied, hoping that he would not ask me any specific questions about the plot because I would be at a loss for answers.

"What's your favorite movie of all time?" He asked, and I could feel my shoulders drop with relief.

"The Godfather, definitely. What's yours?"

"The Godfather," he wondered. "I don't think I've ever seen it."

I stopped in my tracks, causing a ruffle in the traffic going on behind us. "You've never seen The Godfather? Ever?" It came as a shock to me that there are still some people who have yet to see the greatest movie of all time, and I had no idea that Danny was one of those people.

"I'm sorry, but I have not," he admitted, hanging his head.

"I have to admit, I was thinking that this was going well, you and I," I clarified, blushing. "But now, you're telling me that you've never seen one of the greatest movies of all time? Danny, come on, do better," I mocked sarcastically. My smile quickly faded as I remembered Jana telling me not to make any sarcastic comments like I usually do.

"We could watch it together?" He suggested, bringing my smile right back onto my face. I was so relieved that he did not take any offence to my sarcastic remarks.

"I like the sound of that," I replied softly, squeezing his hand and pulling myself closer to him. He squeezed my hand tighter once again as we continued to walk in and out of every store we passed by. I wanted to stay here forever; this did not seem real.

"I'm sorry I took so long to tell you how I felt about you," he whispered quietly into my ear. My heart skipped a beat and I thought I was going to explode with excitement.

"We're here now," I assured him, matching his whispered hush. I wasn't quite sure why we were whispering, but I didn't mind.

"I like you, a lot," he said as he spun me around so I was facing him. My cheeks were flushed, and I could feel my palms start to get sweaty. I wanted to stay in his arms forever, I wanted to tell him that I liked him very much, but before I got a chance, his lips were on mine. This time it was not as awkward as yesterday, but it was rather passionate; meaningful. His arms were resting around my waist as he pulled me closer towards him.

Being in his arms felt safe, and I had no worries. I had never felt like this before, and I did not know what this feeling was. This feeling of excitement, happiness, but yet uncertainty, was making my head hurt.

"I won't break your heart," he said quietly into my ear.

"I know."

I knew it was a lie, however, I knew that men always broke my heart. Instead of listening to my head, I remained vulnerable in his arms, knowing that one day I would regret this.

Chapter 19

"I saw your Instagram post," Tony teased me. Tony, Luca and myself were on FaceTime because we hadn't in a while.

"Me too," Luca said plainly. This was awkward. Luca hasn't said anything bad about Danny, but it was still awkward to talk about him with Luca.

"I like that post," I defended. Danny and I posted a picture of the two of us with our cheeks pressed tightly together with bright smiles on both of our faces; I loved that photo.

"Have you guys kissed?" Tony pressed, raising his eyebrows high. I didn't want to tell them, especially because things were still awkward between Luca and myself, but my facial expression said it all.

"You have!" Luca smiled, but I could tell he didn't like that.

"You're blushing!" Tony let out a lengthy laugh. I just rolled my eyes and didn't say anything because it really wasn't any of their business.

"You're just jealous because you don't get past the first date," Luca teased Tony.

"This is true." He nodded, not seeming fazed by Luca's comment at all.

"So," Luca started, getting very serious all of a sudden, "are you able to focus on Insieme now that you have a boyfriend?"

"Of course," I responded almost too quickly. The truth is, I haven't given Insieme that much thought ever since Danny. It wasn't that I didn't want to get famous anymore, because everyone knows that I still want that, but I just got wrapped up in the excitement of being in a new relationship. All my thoughts, all my actions, all my words, were wrapped around Danny.

"Danny won't mind that you're hanging out with us?" Tony questioned spetically.

"No, he's seen all of our videos." I shook my head.

"He doesn't have a problem with you hanging out with the two of us?"

"No, Tony, he's fine." My voice started to sound stern, and I barely recognized it. The boys noticed my change in tone and decided to switch the topic back to school. We talked for about four hours before I decided to go to bed. I told them that I was extremely tired and worn out, and I left the call.

I was already in my pajamas when I heard a faint knock on my door.

"Come in." My mother appeared with a note in her hand, and I was silently hoping it was from Tony.

"Hi, you have a letter from Tony," she said, plopping the unopened envelope down on my desk. She stared down at my desk, debating whether or not she should say what was on her mind. "So, this boy," she started, and I could feel my whole body tense up, "do you really like him?"

"Yeah," I blushed, staring down at my carpet.

"I just don't want you to get hurt."

"I won't," I promised, but my mother did not say anything. She gave me this weird look, and then immediately said goodnight, leaving me all alone. I decided I would ask her about it in the morning, and I tore open my letter.

Giovanna,

What a nice surprise! How did you know that I love letters? I am flattered that you think so highly of me, and I am so glad that I bumped into you at Lane's as well. I love you with all my heart and I would do anything for you, anything at all. To be honest, I don't quite know what the future has in store for us, but I know that I want you to be a part of my life. I feel like I can be completely honest with you, but I haven't been. Please text me when you get this so I can come clean.

Love you lots,

Tony.

My heart started to race as I quickly grabbed my phone. I thought that Tony and I had built a relationship strong enough for us to be completely honest with each other, and now he's telling me that he hasn't been. I felt hurt. Betrayed. I let him see me cry and even wrote him a nice letter, and I don't really know what kind of response I was expecting, but it wasn't Tony telling me that he's keeping secrets from me.

Me: I just got your letter. I love you, but what do you need to tell me?

Tony: Can you come over?

This was serious, and all my anger flushed into worry as I woke my mother up and jumped into the car. I let him know that I was on my way and my mother told me to stop bouncing my leg, but I couldn't. I was so nervous and concerned for Tony. Finally, my mother dropped me off at his house and told me just to sleep over at his place and screeched off onto the street. I banged on the door, not caring if I woke the whole neighborhood because this was one of my best friends.

"Tony!" I yelled as soon as he opened the door. I flung myself into his arms and for some reason I started crying. I didn't even know what was wrong, but I had this feeling that it was something bad.

"Thanks for coming on such short notice," Tony said, leading me into his basement. "Can I get you anything to drink?"

"No, I'm fine, thanks." My voice was wobbly, and then I went silent. I didn't realize that Luca was over. "Hi."

"Hey," he gave me a tired smile.

"When you told me that you were coming over, I told Luca to come over so I could tell him as well," he explained, and that made me feel a little better that I wasn't the only one who didn't know whatever Tony had to say. "Please, sit down." He gestured towards the couch and I plopped down next to Luca. Tony was pacing back and forth nervously in front of the couch.

"What's going on, Tony?" Luca asked, his voice barely a whisper.

"You guys are sleeping over, right?" He deflected.

"Yes," I answered for the both of us. "Tony, it's alright, you can tell us anything."

He let out a big sigh, "I don't know how to say it."

"T, we love you. I am positive that we will understand whatever it is you need to tell us," Luca reasoned sympathetically.

"I'm gay."

Oh.

"Say something," he pleaded, his voice cracking.

What was I supposed to say? Luca looked just as shocked as me. I didn't see this coming. But then again, what was I expecting? I had nothing to say to him, so instead of ensuring him that I didn't care who he loved because I still loved him, I got up and embraced him tightly. I could feel his tears staining my sweatshirt, but I didn't mind.

"I love you." I squeezed him tighter. "You know that it doesn't matter to me, right?"

"I should have told you sooner," he cried, burying his head further into my shoulder.

"It doesn't matter. It's a hard thing to say, and thank you for sharing it with me."

Luca gave him a hug as well. "That's very brave of you to tell us."

"How about we celebrate with a drink?" Tony proposed, but didn't wait for an answer as he made his way over to the fridge and pulled out three beers. "Here's to me," he toasted.

"Here's to you," Luca and I repeated, looking at him with proud smiles.

Chapter 20

I don't remember how many drinks I had, but I know that it was well over four. Although, this morning I could recall every event that took place last night. I remember Tony coming out and us dancing the night away, and I certainly remember not kissing Luca this time.

It all made sense now. Tony would always show up to functions single, he's never been in a serious relationship, and I don't think I've ever heard him talk about a girl he's interested in. Good for him. Insieme definitely got closer after last night, and now that I was at home I realized that I missed the two of them a lot, and that's why we were just going home to freshen up and then seeing each other really soon. We planned on doing another cover video for our channel, since none of us could come up with any original lyrics. Before I headed back over to Tony's house I picked up my phone to call Danny. Things were going pretty well between us, and I was hoping that it would stay that way.

"Hi, Giovanna," Danny said happily.

"Hey, what are you up to?"

"Nothing. I was wondering if you were free tonight, I could pick you up and you could come over to my house."

"I would love to, but you would have to pick me up from Tony's house because we're making another video. Is that alright?"

"Sounds like a plan, see you later."

"I'll text you the address," I mentioned before ending the call. We usually don't talk on the phone for long periods of time, and I didn't really mind that. My dad told me to hurry up and before I knew it, I was in his truck. I told him all about my plans with Danny.

"You can stay the night because your mother and I are going to be working late and your brother is busy," he said.

"Really?" I was taken aback. My dad has been laid back about the whole Danny situation, but I didn't expect him to be this laid back.

"Yeah," he said nonchalantly. "Just be careful."

"I am protecting my heart," I assured him.

"No, I'm not talking about that."

"Dad!" I yelped, my face turning four shades of red. Thank goodness we were just outside of Tony's house before he could say anything more.

"Come on, we're going to record right away." Tony grabbed my arm and pulled me inside. His phone was already set up and ready to go and Luca was waiting patiently downstairs. We did one practice round of our cover of *No One* by Alicia Keys before we filmed our final take. We sounded amazing together, and this time I did not pass out or drop to the ground. I was too excited about going to Danny's house tonight.

"Danny is picking me up soon," I rejoiced once Tony had finished uploading our video to our channel. Our other videos had over twenty thousand views now, putting me in an even happier mood.

"What are you guys doing?" Tony jeered.

"He's taking me to his house," I laughed. "Speaking of."

The three of us went to the door as soon as we heard the doorbell. I opened the door to find my handsome boyfriend standing there. He was wearing black jeans that rolled up once around his ankle, a navy blue button up shirt with the top button undone to reveal his chest, and black slip on vans. He was also wearing the simple gold chain that he wears everyday to school, and I couldn't help but smile.

"You must be Danny," Luca bleated, extending his hand out to shake. Tony did the same, but he was much more welcoming than Luca.

"Let's get going," I said to Danny, not wanting Luca to be around him anymore.

"Is everything alright?" He asked me, opening the door to his mother's car. I was in no mood to put up with his mother's cold attitude today.

"Hello, Ms. Garcia," I acknowledged, ignoring Danny's question. I got no response, but rather just a glare in return.

"Aren't you going to say hello to Giovanna?" Danny asked, clearly upset with his mother's behaviour.

"Hello, Danny," she mumbled. That was it. One of my best friends just came out to me and nobody was going to ruin my good mood. Perhaps I was a bit mad because Luca was being awkward about my dating situation, but that's besides the point; she had to be put in her place.

"Mrs. Garcia," I started, and I could feel Danny's hopeful eyes on me, "I have had a weird past couple of nights and I don't want to put up with your rudeness today." Maybe I should have been more polite, but I didn't care right now. "The least you could do is at least say a simple hello to me when I enter your car."

"Do you want to know why I don't talk to you?" She asked, and I nodded my head and raised my eyebrows in anticipation. "I don't talk to you because I know my son is too good for you."

Silence fell over the SUV, and my mouth was so far open to the ground that a fly could enter. "I've seen your little YouTube videos," she sneered. "I can already tell that Danny deserves better."

"Haven't you noticed how much happier I've been now that I'm with Giovanna?" Danny budded in.

"Why can't you see that she's using you!" She yelled, and I could feel the anger well up inside me. "She's clearly dating one of the boys, probably the one with the darker hair," I knew she was talking about Luca. I wanted to tell her how wrong she was, even though Luca claims that the two of us have chemistry. "She's using you to make herself feel better because none of her videos are going viral and she needs to feel loved."

"You don't know me!" I challenged, inching closer towards her from the back seat, placing my elbows on my knees. The words came out of my mouth before I had a chance to think about a more responsible way to handle her. "I don't need a man to feel loved, no offence, Danny." I turned to him, but he shrugged it off. "I have liked your son since the day he walked into my science class, and when he asked me out I was thrilled beyond words." I could feel a smile come across my face as I thought back to the first time I saw Danny. "I'm not dating Luca, you know, the boy in my video, and I don't need your approval. I have no idea what I have done to make you hate me, and quite honestly, I really don't care." I heard Danny laugh under his breath, but quickly stopped after he received a glare from his mother in the rearview mirror. "So, when someone comes into the car, be an adult, and say hello." I leaned away from her, and I was proud that I finally got that off my chest. I truly did not care at this point if his mother liked me or not because I know that Danny and I will be okay no matter what.

The rest of the car ride to his house was silent, and when Danny led me to his basement I was glad that she was no longer with us. His basement looked like a movie theater with his pot lights that dimmed, leather reclining chairs, and movie posters hung up on every inch of the walls. "Sit down, I'll go get us something to drink," he instructed before he left the room. I was very nervous, but I was even more excited to spend time with Danny.

"Here you go." Danny passed me a bottle of carbonated water as he sat down beside me.

"How'd you know that I love carbonated water?" I asked, taking a big sip.

"I overheard you in science class," he explained, sliding closer to me. "You look beautiful."

"Thank you," I blushed, but I managed to maintain eye contact with him. "I really like your outfit."

"Come here," he whispered gently into my ear and cupped my face into his hands. He placed one of my curls behind my ear before our lips met. I placed my hands around his neck as he leaned closer to me, his hands now low on my waist. I quietly lowered myself onto my back, pulling him down with me.

He was breathing heavily around my neck and ear, which made me smile. His gold chain was dangling loosely around his neck and he would stop ever so slightly to look into my eyes. I felt like I was walking on sunshine, and I never wanted to leave. I could lay there in his arms for days on end, but he pulled away.

"I have something for you," he said, giving me a shy smile as he reached for the side table next to the chair. My heart raced with anticipation as I patiently waited for him to reveal his gift. "I bought this," he stated, revealing a DVD cover of *The Godfather*. I gasped and clasped my hands together.

"You remembered," I whispered in shock. I wanted to give him a big hug, I wanted to tell him how much his simple gesture meant to me. I was at a loss for words, but I somehow managed to muster up a smile.

"Of course I did," he said as he made his way over to insert the disc. "We're watching it tonight."

As soon as he returned to the couch he wrapped me up and our lips met again. This time was even more passionate than the previous, and I could feel the electricity between us. I twisted myself until I was on his lap, and he gripped my back gently, but tightly. We were inseparable, and I liked that. I liked how his hand fit on mine, I liked how our lips fit perfectly together, I just liked him. I watched Danny closely as he went over to get us another bottle of carbonated water. His hair flopped in front of his eyes with every step he took, his once freshly ironed button up shirt was now creased with tiny wrinkles all over. His arms were not too muscular, but they were toned. I watched as he carefully examined each of the flavours of water in his refrigerator, carefully placing any bottle back that did not satisfy him. I felt stupid admiring him, but I couldn't help myself. I wanted to look away, but my eyes remained peeled to him.

"Do you want lime or cherry?" He asked as he approached me with two different flavours of water in either of his hands.

"I'll take the cherry flavour, please."

"Thank goodness, I hate cherry," He sighed, groaning as he sat down again.

"Sore?" I smirked.

"My workout was intense yesterday," He admitted, looking over at me but saying nothing more. We sat there watching the previews for what felt like hours, but I did not mind staring into his deep brown eyes.

"What'd you do in your workout?" I asked finally. He explained everything to how many sets and reps he did while I listened intently. Sometimes I would lose focus on what he was saying because I got lost in his looks. Everything seemed right. Everything felt right.

"I'm gonna turn on the fireplace," he announced once he was finished telling me about his tough workout he did yesterday. He flicked on a switch and red flames emerged from the big brick fireplace. I heard the faint sound of *The Godfather's* theme song come on, and now the movie had my undivided attention.

The only time we spoke to each other was when the movie would switch to Italian and no longer had English subtitles so I had to translate it for him. I was surprised at how focused Danny was on the movie, and I, of course, had my eyes locked in on the TV screen. Once the movie was over, we discussed our favourite parts and our favourite characters. I excused myself to the washroom, realizing that I need to check in with my dad.

Me: Hey dad, everything is good. I just wanted to check what time you are picking me up?

Dad: Glad to hear, but I thought we discussed that you are spending the night there?

My face lit up with excitement, but I wondered if it bothered him that I was spending more time with Danny, but I did not question him.

Me: That's right, sorry. I love you.

Dad: I love you, too. Text me if you need anything.

"Is everything alright, Giovanna?" Danny asked, faintly knocking on the bathroom door.

I swung the door open, "I can stay the night!" I beamed. Before I knew it, he had picked me up and I had wrapped my legs around his waist and my arms draped around his neck. He gently placed me on top of the countertop while he playfully kissed me. I pulled myself closer to him, longing for his presence, and squeezed his neck tighter after every kiss.

He scooped me up, still kissing me, and brought me back over to the couch. We stayed wrapped around each other for the rest of the evening until we eventually fell asleep on top of each other.

Danny was snoring faintly while I was wide awake, but he awoke to the sound of my phone ringing.

"Hello?" I said weakly, not bothering to see who was calling me before I picked up.

"Giovanna, I need you," A frantic voice on the other line pleaded.

"Lorenzo?" I asked, shooting straight up and almost punching Danny in the face by accident.

"Can you come over?" His voice grew more worrisome after every word he spoke.

"Can we just talk on the phone? It is late-"

"Come over." He hung up, and I sat there for a few minutes trying to process what had just happened. It all seemed strange, I knew that Lorenzo looked up to me, but why was I the one he was calling late in the evening when something went wrong?

I convinced Danny to drive me to Luca's house and we were there in no time. Despite hating driving, Danny drove me without asking what was going on. I instructed him to stay in the car while I saw what was happening. I was furious that I had to leave the comfort of Danny's arms just to check on Luca, but Insieme comes first.

I gently knocked on their door and Lorenzo flung it open right away. I marched in immediately, and unintentionally started interrogating Lorenzo, "What's wrong? Who got hurt? Are you alright?"

"Upstairs." He pointed his finger to the sky, not saying anything more. My heart raced, and I instantly knew it had something to do with Luca. I sprinted up the stairs and tried to find any bad signs. And then I heard it. A shrieking noise coming from his bedroom. I slammed open his door, not asking permission to enter, instantly gasping in shock as I saw him.

Luca was sitting on the ground, unable to control his tears, and when he looked at me, his eyes were bloodshot.

I scooched towards Luca. "What is going on?" I asked, forcing him to meet my gaze. He tried to speak, but only continued to cry louder. His red eyes stared at me, his arms covered with scratches, his clothes wrinkled and tear-stained; it pained me to see him like this. "Pull yourself together!" I demanded, trying to use the tactic of tough love, even though I was on the verge of tears myself.

"I-" he started, but a fresh set of tears streamed down his cheek. I instructed him to take a few deep breaths, which seemed to calm him down a little. "I can't take it anymore." I collapsed myself onto him, well aware of what he was implying. I pushed his head into my arms in hopes that it would comfort him. I constantly cradled him in between my arms, quietly whispering that everything will be alright.

"Don't leave," he said, pulling me down when I got up to go get Danny. "I just want to talk to you."

"Okay." We sat there, me holding him in my arms, in silence forever. "What's going on?" I hushed quietly, still handling him with care.

"What's the point?" He asked, finally looking up at me. I wish he had not looked at me, though, because now I could clearly see his tear stained face and his eyes seemed to have turned a deep red. *What have I done?* I constantly asked myself. I remained silent because I could not find the right words. I had no idea he was feeling this way, and I felt stupid because I hid my dark thoughts in grade eight, so I should have known that Luca was hiding.

"I'm sorry," I managed to spit out, but I choked on the words. My throat was tight, as if a rope was tied around my neck. I knew those two words would not make this situation any better. I could feel the tears start to well up in my eyes, and I did not know what to do. Luca remained silent, making me feel even worse about myself. I wanted to lock myself in a room and never come out.

"I thought we were family." His words hit me like a truck. The words stung my heart, and I could feel the tears streaming down my cheeks. I wanted to stop; I wanted to be strong for Luca. How was I supposed to be strong when I know that Luca doesn't want this anymore because of me?

"We are family." I mustered up the courage to finally say, but Luca just shot me a side-eyed glance. His eyes said a million words, and I knew that things would never go back to normal.

"Give it a rest, Giovanna." His words were tough and distant. "Everytime things start to get rough, you leave. You flip out on those who care about you. You are a coward." I was taken aback by his words, trying to process if he really meant it. I was now standing at one side of his bedroom, Luca on the other. I wanted nothing more than to have things go back to normal. I longed for the feeling of being best friends with him again.

"I know." I hung my head, unable to meet his death stare. I did not want to argue with him anymore, besides, I knew he was right. Whenever things get rough, I leave, simple as that.

"I cared about you. It was me who agreed to make your stupid dream come true!" He was now screaming and I was certain Lorenzo could hear him. "Do you really think that a little girl would come up to you and ask if you wanted a picture because she is a huge fan if it weren't for me? No!" His arms were flailing around and his face was tomato red. "Do you think you would have over ten thousand views if it weren't for me? No!" He now started to approach me, I tried to step back, but he now had me pinned against the wall. "If it were not for Tony and myself, you would be nothing." I could see his nostrils flare with every word he spoke. I could also feel the pain welling up inside me, and I felt helpless. "I can't believe how stupid I was to actually think that you cared about me," he continued, "when all you care about is yourself. For once in my life, once, I felt like I had somebody who understood me. I was wrong. Looking back, I can't believe how blind I was." He paused for several minutes before he moved in closer to me and whispered harshly, "I loved you."

I could not hold it in anymore, my tears rushed out of my eyes like a waterfall. I did not know who this Luca was anymore. I was prepared to help him, I came at midnight to calm him down, but I was not expecting this.

"I love you like a brother, but nothing more," I sniffled.

"Why won't you give me a chance?" His words pierced through his entire house.

"You need to accept the fact that I'm with-"

He kissed me before I could finish. A long, passionate kiss.

My lip was trembling as I pushed Luca off of me and rushed out of his bedroom. I ran down the stairs, tripping over my feet every so often. I caught sight of Lorenzo through my teared lens, but I could not bring myself to speak to him. I turned around to close their front door and I saw Luca. He was standing at the top of his staircase, gazing down at me with such a furrowed expression. I no longer recognized him. I realized that we were now strangers with a few memories, and nothing more.

"Is everything alright?" Danny asked, but didn't press any further when I remained silent. What was I supposed to tell him? That the person I spent most of my time with kissed me?

"Thanks for driving," I whispered as he pulled into his driveway.

"No worries." He led me back downstairs and I simply told him that Luca was just dealing with a lot of emotions right now, which wasn't a total lie.

"Sorry that our night was ruined."

"Don't be," he said sympathetically. "Is there anything I can get you?"

Yes. There was only one thing that could take my mind out of all that was going on in my life right now. Something to make me loosen up and forget about all the bullshit.

"I need a drink."

Chapter 21

One turned into two, two to three, three to four, four to, well I lost count. I felt my soul leave my body with every sip I took. The sweet taste of alcohol made me bubble with excitement every time it touched my lips. Danny didn't drink, not even one.

"Are you sure you don't want one?" I hiccuped as I made my way onto his lap. I had no idea what time it was, nor did I care.

"I'm good," he smirked, pulling me closer to him. The whole room was spinning, and to be perfectly honest, I grabbed onto his neck for balance rather than trying to be romantic.

"Have you ever been in love?" I slurred my words.

"Where is this all coming from?" He sounded concerned, but I just laughed in his face.

"Exactly, we can't be in love if we are only sixteen," I reasoned with Danny. I was trying to make sense of how Luca could have such strong feelings for me.

"Well, I think I love you."

"No you don't," I whispered into his neck. There was no possibility of love at our age. I've learned from experience.

"How do you know that?"

"Can we talk about this in the morning?"

"You're so drunk right now," he smiled, but dropped the subject.

"Perhaps," I giggled.

"Do you always drink this much?" He got serious as I cracked open another bottle. I didn't bother answering him because I was too busy chugging down the sweet taste of my beer. "Giovanna."

"What?" I stared off into the distance. Even though he was sitting right in front of me, my vision was blurred so I couldn't even make out his features.

"You can't handle this much."

I scoffed, "You don't know what I can or cannot handle." I widened my eyes to try and focus back in on him, but it was hard.

"You're sixteen for crying out loud! Maybe you can have one drink. Maybe," he emphasized. "This can't be good for you."

"What is good for me?" I stood up, a little too quickly so I stumbled backwards. "What is good for me, Danny? To deal with all the pain?" I was now yelling at him, and I wasn't sure why.

"I don't know," he whispered. "I just don't like to see you like this."

My eyes felt heavy as I gawked. "Like what."

"This," he motioned his arms towards me. "Look at you!" He dragged me to his bathroom and forced me to look at my reflection. My clothes were messed up, my curls had come undone, my skin was as white as snow, which accentuated the dark circles under my eyes.

"I think I look hot," I joked. That was a lie.

"Why are you doing this to yourself?" He was standing behind me, placed his hands on my shoulders and rested his chin above my head.

At first, I drank for fun. Whenever I would have a sleepover or I was hanging out with a couple of friends I would have a few drinks here and there. Now, however, it takes my mind off of everything. My life was so simple before Insieme, before Luca. I don't know how to deal with all the stress and all the drama, so I drink. I drink until I

can't feel my face, until I don't even recognize
myself.

"I don't know," I answered. "I'm tired." I
wasn't, I could keep drinking, but I didn't want to
talk to him anymore. He wouldn't understand, he
would judge me.

"Come on." He spread his arms open and I
allowed myself to be carried by him. He brought me
over to the hideabed and gently placed a blanket
over me. He softly kissed my forehead and
whispered some words that I couldn't quite make
out, and I fell into a deep sleep instantly.

"Shit." I sat up and took a deep breath; there
was no way I would show Danny that I was hung
over. I don't remember anything from last night, just
that Luca and I got into a big fight. Oh, and that he
kissed me. My head was pounding, so I shook
Danny awake.

"Goodmorning," he groaned. His voice was
tired and deep, and I just stared at him for a few
minutes. "How are you feeling?"

"I'm good." I leaned in to give him a kiss, but
when our lips touched, it felt distant. There was no

love between us. All those days I would spend daydreaming about dating Danny all seemed silly to me now. I faintly remember him saying something along the lines of him loving me, but then why was it so awkward this morning.

"Are you hungover?" He pulled away from me.

"No, I need to go."

"Is everything alright?" Now he sounded concerned. Where was that two minutes ago?

"Yeah, I just need to be home right now." That was partially true, I needed to go home and shower and put on the cutest dress I could find and then do what I should have done from the start.

Chapter 22

"Where are we headed?" My dad asked me once I was back in his car. I showered and put on my pistachio green dress with white flowers on it, and I even put on a little bit of mascara.

"Luca's house."

The rest of the car ride was dead silent, which I didn't mind because I actually got a chance to write a song. My dad was trying to look at the napkin I was writing on, but I just laughed in his face and shielded it.

Turning on the radio, hearing our song

Wondering where I went wrong.

That could work. My heart was pounding as I tried to come up with the next lyrics.

Once upon a time we were making memories

And now you tell me you don't ever want to see me.

It was pretty simple, but I was proud of it.

I close my eyes and only see you

Now I'm longing for the spark we once had

And now there's nobody to blame but me

I'll admit, I was wrong.

Maybe it was bad, but at least it was something.

Now I'm up all night

Trying to remember our fight

Can't you see that without you I'm nothing?

Please just come back to me

"We're here." My dad interrupted my song writing, but I was so excited that I barely said goodbye to my dad.

I knocked three times on his door and patiently waited for somebody to answer.

"Hi." Giancarlo hugged me immediately. "He's downstairs."

I don't know why I was running, but I was. I was holding the napkin tightly, until I saw him playing video games, then I unintentionally dropped it.

"Giovanna, what are you doing?" He looked concerned; I was concerned for myself. I jumped into the safety of his arms and kissed him without a second thought. He wrapped me up and kissed me back with such passion that it was overwhelming.

"I'm sorry," I whispered into his ear and squeezed him tightly.

"It's alright, you're here now," he smiled at me.

"I have something to show you," I said as I went to pick up the napkin I had used to scribble down the lyrics that came to me on the drive here and handed it to him. He read it, smiled, and then instantly called Tony.

Tony was over in seconds, he claims that he ran here,and Luca made him read my song.

"I love it!" He exclaimed. "I love it, I love it, I. Love. It." So dramatic.

"Do you think Tony loves it?" Luca turned to me and we both shared a length laugh.

"Is everything okay between you two now?" Tony asked. Luca must have told him about our fight, but I didn't mind, it was in the past.

"Yeah," I assured him. "So I was thinking that we should call my uncle's restaurant to see if we can book a gig there."

"Yes!" Luca shouted, and then gently clasped his hand over his mouth and blushed. He was so cute.

Luca picked up the phone and waited for the restaurant to pick up. "Hello, this is Luca Fonzo calling, is the owner there please?" We could all hear the employee say that she needed to put him on hold, so that's why we all rolled our eyes, but then my uncle got on the phone and Luca froze and handed the phone to me.

"Hey, Zio." I shot Luca a death stare but then smiled immediately. How can I stay mad at him? Shit. Is this what love feels like?

"Hi, bella, how are you?"

"Zio, I need to ask a huge favour from you."

"Is everything alright?" I could hear pots and pans clinging in the background, so I decided to get straight to the point.

"You've seen Insieme's Youtube videos." I knew this because he called my mother to congratulate me. "And now we are wondering if we can sing at your restaurant." There was a long pause, and the boys stared at me with anticipation. "Okay." I hung up the phone.

"What'd he say?" Tony questioned.

"What's going on?" Luca pressed.

"Luca, get your guitar," I smirked. "We have a gig to play tonight."

Chapter 23

We spent hours finding the perfect soft melody for our song. We decided to call it *I Was Wrong*, it was a bit basic, but it was still nice. We mastered it, and I was convinced that we could perform this song in our sleep.

Giancarlo said that he would film it and that he already told the rest of our parents to meet us there. I was excited that we could make another portion of my dream come true, and I was even more excited to have my first real performance. Then I realized that I haven't kept Mary updated at all so I decided to send her a quick text.

Me: The last few days have been a gongshow, but we booked a gig tonight at Zio's restaurant and it would mean a lot to me if you could watch? We're doing a few covers and then we will be performing our original song.

Mary: Of course I will be there! Also, don't even worry about not texting me in a few days, I know how life can get. See you soon, love you!

Me: I love you, too.

See, my best friend understands me, and hopefully she will be understanding that I was about

241

to dump Danny. I was dreading it. Well, sort of. Luca and I haven't exactly said that we are official, but all I know is that I feel more of a connection between Luca and I than I do with Danny.

"Giovanna, I have something for you," A little voice peeped from the stairwell. I instantly hugged Lorenzo and apologized for what happened the other night, but he told me not to worry about it and that he was fine.

"This is for you," he said as he handed me the vibrant blue bag.

"Thank you!" I quickly tore open the bag and found what looked like a jewelry box. I gently picked it up and instantly gasped as I recognized the *Silvio Gold* logo, my favourite Italian goldsmith in the city, and I carefully opened up the box. I was speechless when I saw the gold bracelet. I stared awestruck at the beautiful, simple, perfect bracelet; it was so mesmerizing. "I..." I started, but trailed off as I stared closer at the bracelet and noticed that my name was ingrained in cursive. "I love it," I breathed, unable to think of anything else to say.

"Put it on!" Lorenzo insisted, and I obediently clasped the bracelet around my wrist.

The gold complimented my skin tone and matched my gold chain I wore everyday, which was also from Silvio, perfectly. I thanked Lorenzo profusely for the beautiful bracelet and hugged him tight. I assured him that I would bring him a better gift, rather than just a small cutie pie bear I had gotten him already. He told me that there was no need for me to give him another gift, but I knew it was the right thing to do.

"It'll be like your good luck charm," he blushed. I was at a loss for words, so I hugged him as tight as I possibly could.

"Lorenzo, can you head back upstairs and tell dad that we're ready to go soon, but we have to leave a tad earlier because we have to make a stop?" Luca asked nicely and flashed his brother a smile. For the first time, Lorenzo did not protest and did exactly what his older brother told him to do.

"Where are we going?" Tony urged impatiently.

"Giovanna has to go deliver the bad news to Danny." He stared at me.

Tony gasped, "Did you two finally get together?"

"I guess so," I smiled. Usually, I didn't like people knowing my relationship status, but I didn't mind if people knew about Luca and myself. Besides, according to Tony, we were perfect for each other.

"Let's go," Luca stated.

"I'll meet you guys up there, I need to use the washroom," I said and patiently waited for them to leave.

Once they left, I scurried over to Luca's bar. I looked at various bottles of whiskey, vodka, wine, and tequila; so many options. My hands were shaking as I poured the remaining of my water from my metal bottle down the sink and poured the smooth liquor into it. I went with vodka so people wouldn't be able to tell as easily. I wasn't ready to face Danny sober, let alone perform in front of friends and family sober. No way.

"Giovanna! We need to get going!" Luca called from upstairs.

I was so nervous I felt like throwing up, so I took a big sip of the vodka from my bottle. Much better.

Chapter 24

"I just don't think that we will work out," I explained to Danny who was staring at me as if I had a bird's nest in my hair.

"Is it because I told you that I love you?"

"No, I don't even remember that. I just think that it would be best if we remained friends. I don't know what's going to happen with Insieme, and it's not fair to you to keep leaving you in the middle of the night or dragging you to my friends house." I was trying my best to be sympathetic with him, but I really needed to get back to the car because we might be late.

"Giovanna, I still care about you, and I want the best for you, so I need to ask you one thing."

I nodded, "Of course, anything."

"Do you think I'm stupid?" He placed his hand on his chest.

"What?" I blurted.

"I cracked the door open to his house; I didn't stay in the car. I heard everything."

I gulped, "Oh."

"I heard you get cut off in the middle of the sentence; I know you guys kissed. Now, tell me,

Giovanna, why are you showing up at my doorstep to tell me that we're over? Is it because you're with him now?"

"Danny, I didn't intend for this to happen. I have liked you since the very first day I saw you."

"Answer my question." He folded his arms and leaned closer to me. "Are you going out with Luca."

"Yes," I hushed, shooting my eyes down to the floor.

"What the fuck, Giovanna." He looked disgusted.

"Luca isn't a bad guy, and I'm sorry that things didn't work out between us, but we are better off as friends and just talking about sports," I babbled.

"No," he shook his head, "I'm not talking about that. To be honest, I think you guys are a pretty cute couple together and I wish you and the boys nothing but success in the future."

"What are you talking about then?" Now I was confused.

"Your breath."

Oh.

"I just needed something to calm my nerves," I explained.

"You mentioned you have a gig, you should probably leave now." He sounded so disappointed in me and that made me want to cry.

"Please, Danny, I can explain," I begged him.

"You need help."

"What, you think I'm some sort of alcoholic?" I scoffed.

"Goodbye, Gia." And with that he shut the door. I stood in shock until Tony ushered me back into the car and we were on our way to the restaurant.

I was bouncing my leg constantly, partially because I was worried about having a voice crack in the middle of our performance, but mostly because I was worried my family would also smell the alcohol in my breath. I didn't regret taking it; I needed it.

"Are you alright?" Luca placed his hand on my thigh to stop my leg from bouncing, but that just made the bopping to quicken.

"I'm alright." I took a big swig from my bottle.

"We're here," Giancarlo announced as he pulled into *Pazzo's*. It's now or never.

"Giovanna!" My uncle gave me two kisses on the cheek before he shook hands with each of the boys. He barely asked us how we are doing before he showed us where we would be performing. He had a small "stage", which was really only a tiny platform, with three microphones set up for us. He told us that he shut the restaurant down for an hour so we can do a sound check and rehearse before all of his reservations started making their way through. Before we could thank him he was already on his way back to the kitchen to prepare whatever he needed to.

"Let's get started then," Tony said eagerly. Out of all three of us, he looked the most stressed out, but he did seem excited. We spent the majority of the hour that we had making sure that *I Was Wrong* was ready to go. Time flew by in the blink of an eye, and before I knew it, my uncle was telling me that people were all lined up outside his door. What was interesting, though, is that he saw all of his reservations there, but he informed me that he recognized most of my friends and their families from dance and a handful of highschool students he didn't recognize.

I ran "backstage", which was just to the side of our wooden platform, and reached for my bottle. I drank, and drank, and drank until Luca cleared his throat. I closed my eyes and took a deep breath. My uncle let in the audience and I stared at them blankly, thank goodness we weren't on stage right now because they probably would have thought that I was nervous; which I am, but they don't need to know that. As I looked at the crowd of people I smiled at the sight of Mary and Gabi, and saw everyone else from my dance team. My smile turned into a concerned, but happy, look when I spotted Jana and a few of my other friends. I was even surprised to see Danny wearing a smile on his face. Then I saw her. Sonia. Maybe it was the vodka in my system, but I didn't really care what she had to say tonight because nobody was going to ruin this for me.

"This was how things were supposed to be. My dream said that I would perform at *Pazzo's* and it would go viral." I was giving the boys our little pep talk. "Whether or not that will actually happen, I don't know. All I know is that new beginnings lie in the uncertainty of situations."

"I agree," Luca interrupted me. Tony and I shared a funny glance and laughed at him. I was glad that we were still acting normal, even though there was a crowd of people waiting to hear us sing.

"As I was saying," I smiled, "we were born for this. I want you guys to put your heart and soul into this performance because it may be the only one we get. I know that at the beginning of this journey there were a lot of doubts. Perhaps there are more now, but look at that." I pointed to the crowd of people who were waiting eagerly. "All of those people, our friends, our families, are all here to see us. They will know our name."

"We're going to crush it," Tony agreed.

"There's just one thing I need to tell you guys before we go onto the stage," I continued. "I'm sure you all remember our first hate comment from Sonia." The boys' excited expression faded immediately, so I quickly recovered. "Well, she's here tonight." They sighed simultaneously. "Don't worry, we can prove her wrong."

"What do you mean?" Luca asked, he looked super worried now that he knew Sonia was here.

"We can prove to everyone that we are more than just a trio that sings in a basement and keeps a couple thousand views every once-in-a-while," I beamed. "People can finally see who we really are. Most importantly," I paused and looked directly into both of their eyes. "We're coming for everything they said we couldn't have."

Chapter 25

"Thank you!" Luca raised his hands to the crowd. Every inch of his body was covered with little sweat droplets, and so was Tony and myself. We had performed three songs starting with *Story Of My Life*, followed by *Grenade*, and we just finished *No One*. The crowd seemed to love us, and I was overwhelmed with excitement, so I reached for my bottle.

"This is a song that we recently just wrote," Tony said as Luca started strumming the soft sweet melody on his guitar. The crowd cheered and clapped, making me smile from ear to ear.

This was the life I wanted. I wanted people to get excited when we spoke into the microphone. I wanted people to know our names.

A rush of excitement went through my spine as we got a thumbs-up from Giancarlo, who was ready to film our video that was bound to go viral. Bound to make us famous.

I put the microphone to my lips and started singing the first few lines of the song. I actually felt pretty, despite being sweaty, I loved my outfit. My pale green dress fitted me perfectly, and I knew that

I would look so good in the video when we looked back at it.

My palms were sweaty and sticking to the microphone as we continued to sing *I Was Wrong*. The audience was completely silent, you could hear a pin drop. They were staring at us in awe, and that made me almost forget the lyrics. I was over the moon with myself and the boys.

"Thank you all so much for coming here tonight, it really means a lot to us." This time, it was me who spoke once we finished our song. It was probably the best we have ever sang together, and I was certain that this was only the beginning for Insieme. "We would like to give a massive thank you to our families who have supported us through this journey, and, of course, to our friends who have encouraged us to keep working hard. We love you!"

And with that the boys and I rushed off the stage and made our way to the kitchen.

"Giovanna, I loved your performance so much, but I need you guys to go to the banquet room if you want some space from everyone because we are really busy," Zio said in a rush.

We pushed through a couple of doors and we got lost a couple of times, but we eventually made it to the formal banquet room.

"Oh, I already have the video," Luca announced, pulling out his phone and uploading it to our channel immediately. I took another sip from my bottle, I was running low so I would have to start pacing myself, but it tasted too good to put down.

"How thirsty are you tonight?" Tony commented. The boys gave me a skeptical look and I was praying that they wouldn't find out that I was downing vodka at our first gig.

"I'm sorry," I shrugged, but unfortunately took the bottle away from my lips.

"I think we sounded pretty good," Luca said, looking at my bottle.

"Same," Tony agreed.

"How's our video doing?" I asked curiously.

"Holy shit," Luca cursed under his breath. He showed us his phone that would not stop ringing with notifications. In my dream, this was supposed to be the video that got the most attention, but I was not expecting it to blow up in a matter of minutes. We sat in silence, just watching our views go up by the thousands, when we heard somebody come into the room. We all looked at each other with confusion as Danny walked in.

"Giovanna I need to talk to you," he said, already grabbing my arm and pulling me aside.

"What's going on?" I was too happy to even be mad at Danny right now.

"I just wanted to say that I thought you were amazing up there," he gushed. "I also wanted to tell you that I shared the link to your video onto my Instagram, so hopefully you will get even more views."

"Giovanna, we just hit a hundred thousand views!" Tony called across the room. I smiled at Danny, but then ran to the boys to give them a tight hug, and then I trudged back to Danny because I was being sort of rude.

"Sorry," I said. "Thank you so much, Danny, you didn't have to do that."

He shook his head, "No, I wanted to. I really hope you guys make it."

"It really means a lot to me." I looked down at my shoes. "I'm really sorry that things had to end with us." Although Danny and I were better off as friends, it was still a little sad that the person I thought I wanted to go out with turned out to be just a friend. It's for the best, though, and besides, now I wasn't scared to be with Luca.

"Do they know what's in the bottle?" He lowered his voice.

"No, and it's going to stay that way," I hissed.

"This isn't healthy for you."

I stepped closer to him. "You don't know me."

"Giovanna," he started sympathetically, but I really wasn't in the mood for him to judge me.

"Just stop." I raised my hand and I heard the boys get out of their chairs because they thought I was in some sort of trouble. I loved them. "I'm fine, and I don't need you to parent me. Thank you for sharing our video and thank you for the encouraging words, but I think it's time for you to leave."

He was silent and tried to look me in my eyes, but I just flared out my nostrils and stared blankly at the ground. He opened his mouth to say something, but thought twice and turned on his heels and was gone.

"Is everything alright?" Luca came up to me alone. I jumped into his arms, burying my head in his neck. His arms felt safe, and there was no place I would rather be.

"Why don't we go back to your place?" Tony suggested, making his way over to the two of us. I blushed and immediately untangled myself from Luca's grip. "Oh, don't worry, I've been rooting for you guys to get together for, like, ever."

"I think we deserve a drink after that kind of performance," Luca smiled and was already on his way to his dad's car.

Yes, that is what I needed, another drink.

"Congratulations on all your views!" Lorenzo sprang himself at me as soon as he saw me. "I knew you could do it! I always knew!"

"I love you, Lorenzo," I smiled.

The entire car ride was spent by Luca, Tony, and myself receiving compliments from Luca's family. When we arrived at his house, the compliments still continued, but eventually they went to bed and left the three of us alone.

"J.D.?" Tony raised his eyebrows at us. As much as I loved my Jack Daniels, I shouldn't mix my alcohol.

"How about vodka?" I suggested, and they nodded their heads and Luca got out three shot glasses. He filled them to the rim and we toasted to Insieme, and he filled them, and filled them.

"Shit." He tried to fill our glasses again, but there was nothing left in the bottle. I got up to dance because my favourite song, *Where Them Girls At*, just came on. Surprisingly, I didn't stumble. In fact, I wasn't dizzy at all and I was fully aware of all of my surroundings.

"We don't need anymore." Tony pointed at me and laughed.

I danced my way over to Luca, who was still sitting. "Dance with me," I whispered into his ear.

"No," he laughed and turned off the music.

"Hey! I love that song!" I pouted out my lower lip.

"Who's phone is that?" Tony sat straight up and looked around for what was making that buzzing noise. It was my phone, but I didn't recognize the number that was displayed on the screen. I gave the boys a worried look, but they just simply shrugged, so I answered the call.

"Hello?" I said weakly.

Hi!" A cheerful voice responded. "Is this Giovanna Rossi?"

"Um," I put the phone on speaker as I looked at the boys for approval. Both of the boys gave me a nod. "Yes, who am I speaking with?" My voice was irritably high-pitched, and I wish it would return to its natural state.

"Such a pleasure to finally get a hold of you! This is Samantha with *Reen Management*." My eyes went wide and my heart beated heavily. I grasped onto Luca's arm because I suddenly felt all my alcohol and thought I was going to pass out.

"How can I help you?" I asked as I allowed Luca to lead me to his couch.

She chuckled, "Actually, I was wondering if I could help you. I came across your YouTube channel, and I absolutely love your voice."

"The boys are here as well," I corrected her.

The boys introduced themselves, and I was surprised at how calm the two of them were. I, on the other hand, was unable to control the pitch of my voice.

"So nice to get to speak to all of you guys! Like I said, I came across Insieme's YouTube channel and I am in absolute awe of your guys' work. I think your original song *I Was Wrong* is brilliant. I am very impressed with your guys' stage presence. I also think that you guys can be way more than just a trio singing in a basement, I think you guys can sell out stadiums." The boys and I shared a glance, written on Tony's face was confusement and happiness, and written on Luca's face was excitement and eagerness.

"What are you saying?" I asked, barely able to contain my enthusiasm.

"I'm saying that I would like to be Insieme's manager, and I would be able to sign you guys to a label. Are you interested?" The three of us clasped our hands to our mouths simultaneously, and I swear I saw a tear come out of Luca's eye.

"Can we call you back?" I asked. "We should discuss this before we get back to you with an answer."

"Of course, you know where to reach me."

Chapter 26

Silence. Nobody said a word. This was it, this is what we've been waiting for. This was my dream, and now that it could potentially come true, I was scared. I was scared that I would make the wrong decision, what if Samantha is just winning and dining us right now but really just wants to take our money? If we got one hate comment on a silly YouTube video, imagine all the hate we would get if we actually released an album and started performing on real stages.

A thousand thoughts were swirling around in my mind like a tsunami, and I was certain the boys were feeling the same way. I was still shocked that a manager tracked us down and saw potential in us, it just all seemed so crazy.

"Oh," Luca whispered. That was the perfect word to describe how the three of us were feeling. We wanted this, it had always been our intent to get signed. We started off as a couple of friends who just sang a cover song and got some views on their videos. Now, I was witnessing my dream come to life. I don't know if it was the alcohol or the call I just recieved or both, but I was on a high and I had no intent of coming down anytime soon.

"What should we tell her?" Tony broke the silence, but nobody had the answer to his million dollar question.

"I think we should do it," Luca started. "We have nothing to lose, literally nothing, and this is the dream."

He was completely right. Of course, I know that we are not sitting across from John Feton, but now that possibility didn't seem so bizarre.

"At what cost, though?" Tony countered. "You guys know that I want this just as much as you do, but what about school?" Tony, yet again, asked another question that we did not have the answer to.

"We could enroll in online classes and get our diploma that way," I suggested, speaking for the first time since we received the phone call. "I know that my cousin did that and now she's enrolled in a post-secondary school. I know that Insieme is on all of our minds, but we need to get our diploma just in case it doesn't end up working out."

"That sounds like a great solution," Luca shared. Tony seemed to have liked the idea too and we spent about ten minutes looking into the online courses that we could enroll in. Thankfully, we were able to find courses still available and we enrolled in them.

"Are our minds made up?" Tony asked hopefully, looking at Luca and myself with such ambition. The three of us shared a glance before I picked up my phone.

It felt like infinity before Samantha picked up. ""Hello, this is Samantha with *Reen Management*." The boys and I let out a collective sigh once we heard her voice.

"Hi, this is Insieme," I began. "You know, the group you came across on YouTube. This is Giovanna, Giovanna Rossi, and I'm on speaker phone with Tony and Luca."

"I know who you are," she laughed.

"You have yourself a deal."

Chapter 27

Samantha rambled on and on about our plan moving forward. She informed us that we would have to get on the soonest flight down to California as soon as possible. That was my biggest fear: leaving my family and friends behind.

My family knows that I post all these videos, and they have been so supportive of me, but now I would be leaving them for a long period of time. Of course, they would visit me, but I will miss seeing them everyday, and that's why I was speechless as I looked at my parents and brother sitting on Luca's couch.

The boys and I decided that we should get all of our families together to break the news to them. The three of us were standing in front of them as they looked at us with concerned expressions.

Luca cleared his throat, "Thank you all for coming so soon." I was too drunk to handle this right now.

"Is everything alright?" Susana asked right away.

"Yes, mom." Tony took over. "We wanted to inform you guys that Giovanna received a call from a nice lady named Samantha."

"Who's Samantha?" My mother questioned, and my father gently placed his hand on her thigh in hopes that it would calm her nerves, even though my father looked worried himself.

"Samantha came across our channel, and she claims to be a huge fan of ours."

"Not only is she a big fan, but she's a manager," Luca stepped in.

I decided that I should probably input something, since I was the one who received the call. "Have you ever heard of *Reen Management?*"

All of the parents nodded their heads; *Reen* is a very honourable and recognizable management company. They have work all over the world, and I still felt like I was dreaming because there was no way a big company wanted to sign us.

"She wants to sign us to a deal," I explained. "We agreed."

"What?" All of the parents asked, making the boys and myself take a step back. My heart thumped rapidly in my chest as the room filled with silence. I thought they would be excited, after all, it was them who said they knew we would make it into the big leagues.

"Good for you," my brother said, breaking the awkward silence. Antonio always knew when and where to input his opinion, and I loved him for that. My eyes started to swell up with tears as I thought back to all the countless memories my brother and I shared together. I couldn't leave him, I just couldn't.

"Thank you," I whispered.

"We couldn't pass up an opportunity like this," Tony explained further. Why couldn't we? Was it worth it to leave my family behind? Family comes first.

"Say something," I pleaded after the long pause.

"What happens now?" My father asked. I looked over to Luca, silently asking him to take this one.

"We booked our flight," Luca hesitated.

"You did what?" Anna screeched, making the boys and I take another step back.

"We're leaving tomorrow night; we're going to California," Tony continued. "We've worked so hard for this opportunity, and now, there's nothing holding us back."

"What about school?" Giancarlo pressed. "Are you dropping out?"

I gave a slight smile, "No, we've already enrolled in online classes."

"Are you guys going to be able to handle this?" Susana asked.

"Yes," Luca answered a little too quickly. The truth is, I didn't know. I hoped we could, or else this will collapse right before our eyes.

"Well," my dad sighed, "that's my girl." He got up and hugged me tightly. I laughed into his chest as tears streamed down my cheeks. I was going to miss my rock so much. "I'll be right by your side," he assured me as he gently patted my back.

"I love you," I sobbed. I never wanted to leave the safety of my father's grip. Something about him holding me and reassuring me that everything would be alright, put me at ease.

We spent the remainder of the evening reminiscing about our younger years. The boys and

I continued to give our parents all of the information they needed to know about our plan in the future. Looking at everyone sitting on the living room floor, the room so full of laughter and life, it made it hard for me to leave this all behind. The safe thing to do was to stay here. The boys and I said that we have nothing to lose, but we had everything to lose.

How could we leave our families behind? This was all that we've ever known. I couldn't imagine a life where I wake up in the morning and don't see my family. They helped me through my junior high school years, and now I was telling them that I would be leaving them. Maybe I wasn't meant to fulfill my dream.

But then I caught sight of my brother's eyes. He looked at me with such pride it was unbearable. Everyone was talking, but Antonio and I looked at each other in silence. He must have read the worried expression on my face because he mouthed the word *Go* to me. I chuckled a little because I realized what I had to do.

I knew that if I stayed here I would regret it for the rest of my life, and I need to start living my life with no regrets from now on.

Chapter 28

My parents told me that I absolutely needed to go to Mary's house right away to tell her the good news, and so they dropped me off at her house. I told Luca and Tony that I might not be back for the rest of the night, but they understood. Of course breaking the news to my parents was hard, but I was so nervous to tell Mary. I was unsure of how she would react, and even worse, I was worried that we would lose touch in the future. My legs were shaking as I walked to the front door. I took a deep breath before gently knocking.

"Giovanna!" Mary screamed, jumping into my arms. I hugged her tighter than normal, not knowing if I would ever be able to embrace her again.

"What's going on?" She asked, bringing me into her house.

"I have to tell you something." My voice broke, and she quickly grabbed a tissue to catch the teardrops that were falling from eyes. She gently stroked my hair and told me that whatever I was going through, we would get through it together.

"If you're here to tell me how bad your performance went, let me stop you right there because you guys sounded fantastic and I am so proud of you."

"Mary, Insieme got signed to a record label so Tony, Luca, and I are jumping on a plane and going down to California tomorrow," I blurted, burying my face into her shoulder.

"Why are you crying?" She laughed. "This is great news! I knew you would do it! I always knew; I always believed."

"I don't want to leave you."

"Don't let me hold you back. I need you to know that you will always have a place in my heart; you're always welcome here. I love you, and that's why I'm telling you to go." Her words were filled with compassion, not a single drop of jealousy laced in her words.

"What about everything?" I asked, "What about dance? How can I leave those girls without saying goodbye?"

"I'll take care of it," she assured me.

"Mar, I'm scared. What if this doesn't work out; I'm risking everything. Who will I call when things get rough?"

"Me." She pointed to herself. "You can always count on me because I love you."

"I love you, too."

"Shit, Giovanna, your breath reeks of alcohol," she commented. "How much have you had to drink?"

"Not that much," I lied. "The boys and I just had a few drinks to celebrate."

"So," she changed the subject, "you must be excited."

"What if it doesn't work out?" I asked, worry consuming my body yet again.

"It will." She sounded so certain and I wished I could believe her.

"How can you be so sure?" I countered.

"Because I know my best friend," she laughed. "You've always been determined, and once you put your mind to something, it always happens." There was a long pause and tears threatened at the corners of my eyes again.

"What am I now?" I questioned softly. I thought it was more of a rhetorical question, but my sister had an answer.

"You're just a girl with a dream, but now it's not a dream anymore. You're the girl who takes chances on her dreams and is now seeing the rewards."

She was right. That's exactly who I was. For so many years I have struggled to know what my true identity was, I would put on fake faces in front of people just to hide all my scars. I was lost, so hopelessly lost, and I felt like I was carrying the weight of the world on my shoulders. But now, it was all so clear.

I'm just a normal girl who just so happened to dream about being famous. I'm a girl who is now willing to take a leap of faith outside my comfort zone and experiment with the uncertainty in my life. I'm the girl who isn't quite sure where she's headed, but I know that this is it.

I am the girl with a dream.

.